SALUS
IDYLLIC AVENUE

2.0

CHAD GANSKE

E-book: 978-0-9950071-1-6
Paperback: 978-0-9950071-0-9

Editor: Jen Ryan

Cover Art: M Joseph Murphy
Typeset in *Warnock* at SpicaBookDesign

Printed and bound with www.createspace.com

"If I found in my own ranks that a certain number of guys wanted to cut my throat, I'd make sure to cut their throats first."
~ *Pierre Elliott Trudeau*

"Not in sickness . . . but in health."
~ *The Patron*

TABLE OF CONTENTS

PART IV   **THE FERNS** 1

   2.1   RESEARCH 3

   2.2   ABANDONED 15

   2.3   THE PENDANT 21

   2.4   HOME 28

   2.5   CHECK IN. 33

   2.6   CLEANSING. 39

   2.7   HEALING 43

   2.8   REBIRTH REDUX 47

   2.9   THE BASE 61

   2.10   THE GLASSES 70

   2.11   NEW BEGINNING 75

PART V   **THE PROJECT** 79

   2.12   THE CHAMBER 81

   2.13   WILD CHILD. 89

   2.14   THE COMPOUND 96

   2.15   THE CLASS-5. 107

   2.16   AN ELECTRIC DREAM. 113

   2.17   WAKE-UP CALL 117

   2.18   IRON MAN. 120

   2.19   THE HOWLING 126

   2.20   NURTURING. 131

   2.21   FAMILY 135

PART VI   BREACH **145**

    2.22 BABY ROOM 147

    2.23 AWAKENING. 153

    2.24 INTERROGATION 157

    2.25 A MEMORY 164

    2.26 THE PLAN 174

    2.27 THE FARMS 178

    2.28 CAMOUFLAGE 182

    2.29 PREPARATION 184

    2.30 THE HOME. 188

    2.31 CAPTURE 197

    2.32 THE DOME. 201

    2.33 ACCIDENT 207

    2.34 THE TOUR 213

    2.35 INAUGURATION 236

    2.36 FINALE 238

    2.37 EXTENDED. 241

EPILOGUE 243

POWER ON

PART IV

THE FERNS

2.1
RESEARCH

The man in white scrubs adjusted his surgical mask before resuming the task of penetrating the exterior membrane of the plant's stem with a scalpel. With a steady hand he pressed firmly on the blade but was unable to pierce the skin. He looked across the table at his partner, also dressed in clean white garb, and squinted against the stark glare of the overhead EM tubes. On the breast pocket of his partner's jacket he could make out the insignia of the *Colonial Research Division*—the CRD.

"I can't break through," said the surgeon, a tone of frustration mounting in his voice.

His partner was staring at a computer monitor displaying an array of digital atoms.

The surgeon yanked off his facemask. "What's happening?"

"It's forming abscisic acid," said the man at the computer. "It's a naturally occurring hormone in plants, released in times of stress."

"I know what it is, Doctor Le," said the surgeon, taking a break to wipe his sweaty forehead. "But what does it mean?"

Doctor Le raised an eyebrow. "It means the plant is stressed."

The surgeon set the scalpel aside. "I've had enough of the knife."

"Would you like to switch positions?"

"You know as well as I that the blade is useless."

"The abscisic acid is a sign of progress," said Doctor Le. "We must present results to the Patron or we'll be replaced by Class-5s."

The surgeon shot an uneasy glance across the table before directing his voice toward a speaker nestled in the high ceiling. "Bring out the liquid nitrogen," he called.

Doctor Le smiled. "It's not like you to up the ante, Doctor Eggers."

"These are desperate times, Doctor Le."

Both men glanced toward the door as a female android in a tight-fitting red dress whisked in. Clutched between her delicate hands was a silver canister that shimmered under the hot lights as she approached.

"Here you are, Doctor Eggers," she said, ruby red lips of a seductress parting to reveal a set of perfect ivory teeth.

"Thank you, Alice. That will be all."

The woman held his glance a moment longer before performing a simple curtsey and departing as smoothly as she had come, the scent of floral perfume trailing in her wake.

When she was gone, Doctor Eggers readjusted his face-mask and breathed deeply behind the fabric. "Deploying the liquid nitrogen," he said after a moment.

"Go on," said Doctor Le.

Doctor Eggers steadied his grip on the canister and unleashed a spray of highly concentrated mist from the mouth of the nozzle, soaking the frond as it faded in color from rich emerald to a dull, chalky olive, before reverting to a healthy shade of green again.

The men's eyes met across the operating table.

"It is unprecedented," said Doctor Eggers, lowering the canister. "There's every indication that it still lives."

"Let's shock it with fire," said Doctor Le.

"Now it's you who is upping the ante," said the surgeon.

"I am as determined as you are. Take my place at the computer."

Doctor Eggers changed positions with his partner and found himself immediately mesmerized by the colorful molecules floating and spinning and forming complex patterns on the screen. There was something happening inside the fern at the cellular level that he could not explain, except to say that it was dynamic and beautiful. The shapes seemed to be moving chaotically about, yet there was a definite sense of purpose that was fascinating to watch, and if not for the sound of his partner's voice, there's no telling how long he would have remained transfixed.

Doctor Le shouted toward the speaker in the ceiling. "Bring the flame thrower!"

The surgeon's eyes took a moment to focus back on his partner, the latent imprints of the molecules slowly fading from his retinas.

"As you can see," Doctor Le continued, "the molecular structure mimics plant life in every conceivable way, but the defense mechanism is outer-worldly. It's evolved to withstand the harshest elements and predators. It's nearly impenetrable, but perhaps we've weakened it."

"Where does it come from?" asked Doctor Eggers.

"What we know for sure is that it began to appear in

great numbers in the outer boundaries after the first nuclear war, flourishing in the fallout ash. This species was only discovered inside the colonies over the last few years, likely introduced by smugglers before it went mainstream."

"Is it indigenous?"

Doctor Le shook his head. "Unknown."

The image on the monitor changed once again. New atoms began floating into the frame, surrounding the original molecule.

"There's something there," said Doctor Le. "It's another compound."

"Is it the acid?"

"Look there—" Doctor Le came quickly around the table to get a closer look.

"What do you see?" asked Doctor Eggers.

"Give me a minute. The computer is processing."

"It's morphing."

"No, it's not. New atoms are being produced by the spore."

"What are they?"

The Alice unit entered with the torch and offered it to Doctor Eggers.

"I'll take that," said Doctor Le, before quickly dismissing the android.

Both men stepped far back from the operating table.

"Shall we wait to see how it transforms?" asked Doctor Eggers.

"Why? Let's continue what we've started." He took aim with the device.

Doctor Eggers looked on with anticipation as a monster of flame was set free upon the plant, so ferocious it melted the legs of the table and ate away the metallic top in a matter of moments. With the operating table in smoldering ruins, the men looked at the remains of the fern on the floor, watching as a full green frond spontaneously regenerated from the ash.

Doctor Eggers removed his mask. "Remarkable."

"It restored its original structure," said Doctor Le. "And yet something foreign continues to manifest with every assault. Look here."

Both men stared at the computer monitor, witnessing the introduction of a new set of digital molecules organizing on-screen. The atomic structure was familiar.

"I can't believe it," said Doctor Le. He hesitated.

Doctor Eggers peered at the screen and then back at his partner. "Those are oxygen molecules."

"Very astute observation, Doctor Eggers."

"But how?"

"It seems the stress is causing the plant to photosynthesize."

They stood in silence until the voice of the Patron filtered through the overhead speakers.

"Children, a comet burns brightly in the night sky, blazing a trail that remains in our hearts and minds long after it has vanished. Remember the comet when you consider the sacrifices of those who delivered us to salvation, for no grand achievement comes without a cost.

"To all my children under the dome, it is with unimaginable anguish that I announce the death of the Executive Director of the Personal Associations Division—a man who shone like a spectacular comet and will live on in us all; for he gave his life to defend the Policy so that we should live.

"We owe a debt of gratitude to our fallen hero. He wanted more than anything to watch us flourish in our new home; and he too dreamed of an idyllic time when he could settle into a renewed life and reap the rewards of a society that exists not in sickness but in health . . ."

The message continued on about a memorial service as the Alice unit re-entered the operating room and glanced at the doctors.

"Shall I clean up for you?" she asked.

"No," said Doctor Le. He glanced absently around at the destruction. "We need more time."

The Alice unit nodded before leaving through a rear door marked: *Servant's Quarters: Android Personnel Only.*

Behind the door was a dimly lit anteroom with a dining table at the center. The ceiling was cut with a grand skylight, giving a spectacular view of the protective dome of Salus miles overhead.

Already seated at the table was a woman dressed in an identical red dress, with brown hair cascading over her delicate shoulder blades.

Alice sat down opposite, and the women smiled at one another over a candlelit centerpiece.

"I feel sad," said Alice as she tucked in.

"You don't look sad. You look positively beautiful."

"Thank you. I'm trying to be strong."

"Rumor has it the Director's head was recovered in the boundaries. The body is still missing."

"It's terrible news, but that's not what I've been thinking about," said Alice.

"Please don't be this way," said the other woman. "Let's enjoy our last meal together."

"I just wish you had more time. Aren't you the least bit worried?"

"A little, I suppose. But I know it's for the best. We were designed to live for the Patron. This is a sacrifice I must make as an older generation android. I knew this time would come."

"But you have so much to offer. Why can't they employ you to hold the babies in the nurturing rooms? There are so many children that require care."

The woman hesitated. "I failed to eradicate the mutant's gene, Alice. My time here is over. I'm obsolete."

Alice couldn't mask her grief any longer. Her chin quivered as she took a sip from her water glass. A single tear streaked down her pale cheek. "I will miss you, Glenda."

Glenda smiled. "Look at how advanced you are, Alice. Your tears are the product of genuine human emotion. My emotions were programmed. The Personal Associations Division has come a long way. I feel proud of my contribution to the Policy, but I have no more to give. I'm at peace with that. You are the future."

"No, I'm not. They've already introduced the Class-5 Series. Every year the models become more intelligent. I don't understand why they cull the population of humans and then search for ways to recreate them."

Glenda reached across to touch her friend's hand. "You know why. You are just upset." She stared at the flickering candlelight for a moment before looking back into her companion's eyes. "Tell me something funny. I always love to see you laugh."

Alice feigned an unconvincing smile.

"Please, Alice, tell me something funny."

Alice thought for a moment before feeling a tug on the corners of her mouth. "Well, the doctors in the lab are going to burn down the entire facility trying to figure out that fern."

Both women stared at one another before bursting into laughter.

"So much fuss over a plant!"

"It's good to see you laugh, Alice. Let's enjoy our last meal together, okay?"

Alice nodded. "What are we having for dinner?"

On cue, a sophisticated Gen-3 robot aide entered with a thermal platter of fresh shellfish: prawns, lobster, clams, crab—all pink and succulent and fleshy. The robot set the platter down before revealing a bottle of wine hidden under its metallic arm.

"This looks wonderful," said Glenda. "Thank you."

"It was prepared especially for you," said the aide, pouring the wine. "Can I bring anything else?"

"We're fine for now," said Glenda. "Please thank the chef."

The aide nodded and departed.

When they were alone again, Glenda peeled the shell off a plumpish prawn and swallowed it whole. "I love seafood," she said, smacking her vibrant red lips. "It's so primal to eat flesh like this. It makes me feel like I'm a real human before the war, with access to all kinds of creatures to hunt in their natural habitats."

"I love it too," said Alice. "There is an overabundance of genuine animals for everyone to enjoy inside Salus. We are so lucky—"

She caught herself and immediately cast her eyes downward.

Glenda smiled. "Please don't worry about me, Alice. I'm at peace with this." She raised her glass of wine. "Let's make a toast."

Alice glanced back through bleary vision and elevated her glass. "To Glenda, my dear friend; for all you have sacrificed. You are a true pioneer of the Policy, and a beautiful woman. Hail the Patron."

"Hail the Patron."

The two women clinked their glasses just as a handsome-looking man in a security jacket entered the anteroom. There was a symbol on his lapel: PAD.

"They are waiting for you, Glenda," said the man.

A hush fell over the room.

"Can I go with her?" asked Alice, looking suddenly panicked.

The security man huffed and reached for the transmitter attached to his hip. He spoke into the receiver: "The Alice unit requests permission to accompany the Glenda unit to the disassembling station. Over."

The voice on the other end returned: "Why would she want to do that? Over."

"I don't know," said the security man. "Can she come or not? Over."

There was a short delay in the transmission.

Alice reached across the table to hold Glenda's hand.

The voice crackled back: "If she wants to come, bring her along. It makes no difference. Over and out."

The security man looked back and forth between both women. His pupils constricted to the size of pinpricks. "Let's go, ladies."

The women were escorted to an elevator that shot up several floors before stopping at a garage door labeled: *Disassembling Station.*

The door lifted to reveal a large room resembling an airport hangar. All throughout were massive garbage bins filled with spare parts pulled from older generation androids.

The trio was immediately met by a grungy-looking mechanic dressed in blue overalls with patchy oil stains on the bib.

The security man gestured toward Glenda. "This is the old unit," he said. "And this other one is Alice. She's been given clearance to accompany Glenda to the chop shop."

The mechanic chuckled and wiped his hands with a soiled rag as he looked at Alice from head to toe. "Is she going to read the last rites?"

"Let's just get this over with," said the security man.

The mechanic grunted and gestured for the trio to follow him through the large warehouse.

Alice squeezed Glenda's hand as they crossed the dusty cement floor, arriving at what appeared to be a jail cell located at the far side of the hangar. The cell was empty with the exception of a porcelain sink, a small table holding a chainsaw, and a drain in the center.

The mechanic turned to the women. "I'm sorry, which one of you is Glenda? I can't tell you apart. Maybe I'll just do you both to be safe; like a two-for-one deal."

The security man pointed at the Glenda unit.

"Okay, darling," said the mechanic. "This is the end of the line. Step inside the cell, please."

"Why does she have to go in there?" Alice's voice quivered.

"It's purely precautionary, just in case she decides to bolt."

"But Glenda has no intention—"

The mechanic cut her off. "There's no telling what an android will do when it sees the teeth of the blade. It's strictly procedure."

Glenda pulled her friend into an embrace. "I love you," she said. "I will never forget you."

"I love you too, Glenda."

Tears streaked down both androids' faces as Glenda stepped into the cell with the mechanic.

Alice wiped Glenda's cheeks through the bars with her fingertips. "You have genuine tears," she said softly.

The mechanic bolted the door and took a moment to examine Glenda's sleek figure. "In your final moments, I want you to think about how your beautiful body will be disassembled and used as parts for the Class-5s. Think of this not as a death, but as a reincarnation into something better."

The mechanic picked up the chainsaw.

Glenda backed into a corner of the cell and began to sob. For the first time, she exhibited the terror that she had previously repressed. "Alice," she cried. "Please say the command. Have mercy on me."

Alice reached out to her captive friend, but was restrained by the security man. "Be strong, Glenda. I'll never forget you."

The chainsaw buzzed.

The mechanic looked out the bars toward Alice. "If you're going to say something, you better say it now."

Alice looked at her friend through streaming tears. She spoke the command. "Salvation," she said. "Salvation . . ."

Then Alice closed her eyes.

The keyword command initiated the shutdown feature. Glenda's eyes went dim and her body slumped, completely inert.

Moments later, the chainsaw severed Glenda's head from her torso.

2.2
ABANDONED

A temporary base had been set up in the desert with a view of Salus in the distance. The green mass of ferns encroached on the sides of the dome like an over-fertilized crop of weeds, threatening to engulf it whole. The top of the dome glowed in the night like a beacon, a protective sanctuary for the first inhabitants of the new civilization, and a shining target for the Tech Terrorists.

The physicals had no such shelter. Tents had been erected next to mobile electricity tanks that hummed from the inside out. Campfires were built to fend off the piercing cold of permanent midnight. At some point in the not-too-distant future, the starving flames would flicker and ultimately extinguish for lack of oxygen. The twin suns would no longer come back to reignite the planet.

Stanford kneeled in the sand to give the old boy a good scratch behind the ears. "Sleep well, old boy."

The dog looked up—wide eyes brimming with vitality, and with an incredible burst of energy, the collie barked and shot to his feet, racing into the darkness away from the encampment.

"Where are you going, old boy?" Stanford trained his glowing irises in the direction of the dog.

The old boy paused to look back, standing for a moment at the edge of the spotlight cast by his master's eyes, before darting out of sight.

It was difficult to trudge across the sand. A blanket of nuclear ash lay upon the barren terrain, creating a spongy, unstable surface. As he pursued the old boy, Stanford wondered if he would come across his child out here in the cold. He couldn't imagine what was worse—being alone in the dark or captive inside the dome with the helix dogs. He pictured his child in the incubator, his cries ignored by the strangers who wanted to prod him, to open up his tiny body and see what was inside. Stanford felt a shudder run down his spine. His skin was instantly frigid and taut over his bones.

"Where are you taking me?"

Propelled by adrenaline, he increased his speed across the dunes. Had the dog picked up the scent of his newborn son? His heart thumped in his chest as he followed the light cut by the glowing copper in his mutant eyes. Every time the old boy eluded his sight, the dog would reappear again, as if waiting for his master to catch up.

"Wait for me, old boy. I'm coming."

Stanford felt tightness in his chest. He gasped for breath, but he would not let his body fail him, not with the possibility of locating his child out here amongst the dunes. He imagined finding his boy wrapped in a blanket on the sand, discarded by the beasts who had stolen him. He would bring the child to his breast to warm him, seeing the tiny eyes of Saturn staring back.

You'll be okay. I'm here now. I'll never let you go.

Scanning the desert, he saw nothing but infertile landscape stretched out before him. The farther he ran into darkness, the more he came to realize the unbearable possibility that he was being led into an abyss, with no chance of finding his way back.

"Don't leave me, old boy," he called into the night.

But I left him.

This is what it's like to be abandoned, he thought. He felt like a failure. His boy was out here, and he didn't have the power to rescue him. There was no forgiving that. Now he was alone in this vast, barren existence; just like the old boy, just like his son.

The energy evaporated from his body into the cold, dry air, displaced by a sense of loss and regret. His legs felt suddenly heavy, his shoulders slumped, and just as his pace began to slow, he felt a tug on his foot that caused him to lose balance and collapse in the sand. He lay there for a moment, motionless, tasting the foul ash that dusted his lips. It was vile and made him retch. He had the urge to fill his mouth with the toxic waste and stay in the desert until he suffocated. His body and mind were spent, and if he could not have his son, then death seemed like an appealing alternative. But he knew he would not be permitted to die out here. The physicals would find him and bring him back, just as they had before. He had a mission to fulfill, and no matter how feeble he felt, he would not abandon his son. Now he realized why the old boy had brought him here. He needed to be reminded about the importance of staying alive.

Summoning his strength, he glanced back at the object that had upended him. He focused his eye-beams on a partially exposed humanoid hand with insulated wires for tendons. It protruded from the ground as if it had dug itself out of a shallow grave. It was a piece of the Director's mutilated body that had been scattered across the dunes by the physicals, each part buried where it would decompose in the nuclear ash of Ultim's badlands. The body segments would never be found, never pieced back together, never idolized by the society of Perfects. He watched the hand twitch before spontaneously disintegrating into a puff of dust. It had no place here now.

Stanford felt a fleeting moment of vindication as he turned over, flat on his back, to stare up at the faint twinkle of distant galaxies so many light years away. Somewhere in the star clusters were previous homes of mankind; barren rocks stripped of life, floating in space, long lost and forgotten. The heavens were a black velvet backdrop, empty and lonely. How could Ultim be so utterly alone in the universe? This is where the path of the human species terminated. The expeditions were over, resources spent. They had done this to themselves, orchestrating their own demise without forethought. There was nowhere but here. There were innumerable planets amongst the stars, and this is where it all ended—in the middle of a black, empty pit in space.

If only he could have made a choice to flee to another place—a place that was alive and warm and sustainable; a place not covered over by an artificial dome. But there was no choice. Not now. The suns were gone and they weren't coming back. The humans were stuck here. And they had to share their final resting place with androids. There was the dome or there was death.

Stanford closed his eyes. There was nothing to look at anyway. He imagined himself in a dense forest with the sound of a waterfall beckoning him from nearby. The soothing sound of a frothy cascade wafted across his body, releasing the tension from his muscles. He pictured Sarah wading through the shallow pool toward him, the wet ropes of her dark hair falling down to cover the contours of her breasts.

I love you, Stanford Samuels.

I love you too, Sarah. I'm coming. Stay where you are.

He moved through the tangled bank, and when he pushed into the clearing he saw nothing. Sarah was not there. The waterfall had dried up. Only a faint trickle remained in the cracked mud.

He craned his head toward the canopy, searching for signs of life, but it was silent up high. The only thing that seemed to thrive here were the ferns that grew in abundance on the forest floor. He knelt down to touch a feathery frond, allowing the leaf to wind around his wrist. It circled his arm all the way up to the elbow, prickling his skin like static, putting him at ease.

Bubbles of green energy began to rise off the frond. They made their way into his nostrils, feeding his lungs like medicine. Looking deeper into the forest he saw thousands of bubbles rising off the ferns and floating high above the tallest trees into the atmosphere. The entire forest was cast in a green haze of light. He squeezed his eyelids tightly and inhaled the aroma of plant life. It was pungent but pleasant, opening his alveoli like plump balloons. It was like nothing he had ever experienced. His lungs felt alive in his chest.

Stanford felt something wet on his cheek. When his eyes snapped open he noticed he was back on the desert floor, the old boy's breath warming the side of his face. He turned to watch the dog scamper off into the darkness. There was no catching him now. He knew the old boy didn't want to be caught. He had returned to remind Stanford that the only pain worse than death was the pain of being abandoned.

"Sleep well, old boy," he said, and then he lay back down on the sand and closed his eyes once again.

He pictured the black velvet sky in his mind—a vast, empty canvas.

"Sleep well . . ."

2.3
THE PENDANT

Stanford woke with a start, face plastered against the inside of the van window. The glass was brutally cold. The conditions outside had become considerably more severe in the absence of the suns. It was only a matter of time until sub-zero temperatures hit the colonies.

When his eyes focused behind the double-tinted lenses of his sunglasses, he could see he was traveling down Idyllic Avenue. The Personal Associations Division was in full view through the windshield, the Central Tower sandwiched between two squatty buildings. He felt a shiver run through his body, a combination of both nerves and plummeting temperature.

The tower grew larger through the window, the expansive courtyard vacant behind the iron gates. Even the security androids had joined the mass exodus to Salus after permanent midnight. There were no signs of life, artificial or otherwise.

His head felt thick and disoriented. He couldn't recall how he got here. Turning his attention to the interior of the van, he recognized Joshua and Jack from his previous escort, as well as the figure of the resident mother seated alone in the back seat. There were several other mutants present who he'd never had the pleasure of meeting, but they all bared the distinct characteristics of the physicals. They no longer bothered to cover their deformities with bandanas. Who was there to hide from? He couldn't stare at the oozing pustules and deteriorating flesh any longer. The interior of the van stunk like rot.

As the vehicle rounded the front of the compound, he saw the same gate where he had first met Ilsa K. Her memory crystallized as vividly as if she were seated next to him. He pictured her pale complexion, soft features enveloped by raven black hair that fell upon delicate shoulder blades and traveled all the way down to the small of her back. He remembered her smile most of all. When her lips parted, it was as if she opened her soul to him. Oh, how he missed her smile.

He quickly evacuated her image from his consciousness. The thought of her end was too brutal to consider. He was surrounded by ugliness, and as he glanced at the grotesque faces of the physicals in his immediate vicinity, he realized the mutant assassin who had brought him back from the dead was not among them.

He reached to remove his sunglasses for a better look.

"Leave them on," said Joshua. "You'll make the van light up like a firecracker."

Stanford dropped his hand and stared into the man's face. He appeared to be one of the only mutants spared by the radiation. "You don't look like the others."

Joshua grinned as he unbuttoned his jacket to expose the badly seared flesh of his chest. "Just because you can't see it, doesn't mean it didn't happen."

Stanford looked away. "Where's the assassin?"

"The assassin?"

"The man who took me from my home."

"Are you referring to Markus Dekkar?"

"He never told me his name."

Joshua grunted. "The man you are inquiring about—
'the assassin' as you call him—is back at the camp near Salus.
Do you not remember the base? You insisted that he remain
there while you returned to the colony to say goodbye to your
previous life. You said you needed closure. We decided it was
a good opportunity to do some more scavenging."

Stanford tried to remember, but his mind was uncoop-
erative. For a split second he wondered if he was an unwilling
passenger, steered off course to delay his mission—but he dis-
missed the thought as a product of his semi-lucid state. He
remembered well enough that his relationship with the terrorists was mutually beneficial. They had bonded by necessity.

He stared out the side window to clear his mind, allowing his eyes to absorb the PAD. "Why did we come to this
place?"

"Your memory will come back in time," said Joshua.
"You experienced multiple organ traumas that only a fern
could cure. You said something about making sure your
child wasn't left behind."

Stanford felt a tingling sensation flutter through his
body, as if his flesh was awakening after a period of dor-
mancy. He had the sudden urge to scratch at the wound in
his neck where the I-132 had pierced his jugular. It was a sign
of healing.

"You've been asleep since we left the camp," said
Joshua. "Your body is still repairing. You've been talking out
loud about some dog."

23

Stanford turned to face him. "Is my dog back at the camp?"

"We don't have pets. We don't need more mouths to feed."

The vehicle settled upon the street at the entrance to the Personal Associations Division. The side door opened, introducing a sobering blast of cold air.

Joshua looked toward Stanford expectantly. "Well?"

"Well what?"

"This is your mission. Tell us what to do."

"I'm sorry," said Stanford. "I don't know what you want from me."

Joshua glanced around to address the mutant battalion. "Stand down," he demanded. "I want to talk to Mr. Samuels alone."

The mutants filed out of the vehicle, with the exception of the resident mother who remained silently in the back seat.

Joshua examined Stanford for a moment before leaning in close. "The shaman said it was foretold you would lead us to salvation—a messiah with two burning suns in his eyes."

Stanford felt the copper cyclones swirling in his irises.

"I sense a duality in you, Mr. Samuels. You are running in two directions. One part is determined, but your self-doubt is strong. If I'm going to follow you, I need to know that you are committed to the common goal. Otherwise, it's dangerous for us all."

Stanford looked out the window again, straining to see up to the seventeenth floor of the tower. An image suddenly stood out in his mind, replacing the ugliness with a symbol of innocence. It was his child peering at him through the glass cap of the incubator, the tiny eyes of Saturn mirroring his own. The child was alone in the cold capsule, denied the soft caress of a loving hand. Stanford felt the strong fingers of yearning squeeze his chest.

He removed his glasses and lit the interior of the van.

Joshua shielded his face. "Are you ready for what you might find with those brilliant eyes, Mr. Samuels?"

"I won't abandon my son."

"Lead the way," said Joshua.

Before exiting the van, Stanford glanced at the resident mother in the back seat.

She flinched at the brightness.

Stanford averted his eyes so that she was in shadow again. "You were taking care of a baby," he said. "His mother was not human."

"You remember."

"What happened to him?"

"He's well taken care of. Your only concern should be your own son."

"Will I find my boy up there?"

The resident mother bowed her head. She had no more words.

Stanford looked at her damaged features and saw the answer that she kept hidden. He knew she didn't want to cause him pain. His child was not up there, but he needed to go to the seventeenth floor anyway. He needed to be sure.

The physicals seemed to gravitate to Stanford as he led them toward the building. The iron gates were unlocked. The entrance was no longer guarded by the serpentine camera. All security had been abolished when the main power sources were cut off with the arrival of permanent midnight. There was nothing to protect now.

Memories of his previous visit came back in snippets as Stanford entered the lobby. He looked up at the fresco on the ceiling. It depicted a dense forest cut through by a babbling brook. It was beautiful and serene, showering the guests with a sense of calm.

Is that what it looks like inside Salus?

He signaled the mutants to halt as he made his way down the hallway toward a display case housing a set of six ornate aluminum pendants. When he arrived, he glanced at each pendant as if seeing them for the first time—the eagle, the cobra, the owl, the lion, the moose, and the brown bear; all expertly etched into the aluminum. The freshly polished pendants glinted in the light from his eyes.

Stanford stared at the pendant of the owl, remembering the wall-sized portrait of the Great Horned Owl in Ilsa K's apartment. The recollection created a knot in his stomach, and he leaned on the display case to allow the dizzy spell to pass.

When he stabilized, he stood upright and with a deft act of force, slammed his elbow into the glass and reached through the shards to secure the owl pendant. A shocking alarm began to sound, but nobody came running. The once mighty building that served as the heart of the colonized world had been reduced to a house of relics.

Stanford placed the owl in his pocket and beckoned the physicals to follow. He led them beyond the inoperable elevator to the steep stairwell that ascended the Central Tower. The physicals moved like a predatory snake, winding ceaselessly up the series of stairwells until coming to rest on the seventeenth floor.

They filed into the massive room with the incubators and awaited instruction. Stanford was immediately overcome by grief.

There were hundreds of aisles of empty capsules inside the room, but he knew exactly where his child had slept. The location was etched on his mind just as the owl was etched on the pendant.

He directed the physicals to stand back while he walked deliberately toward the incubator marked by digital number 40065. This is what he had come for. Now he would experience the pain that the resident mother had temporarily spared him.

Through the glass encasement, he saw only his reflection staring back—the copper swirled like a storm in his irises.

He lifted the lid, finding it unlocked, and placed the pendant of the owl on the empty pillow where his child's head had rested.

"This will protect you," he whispered. His mutant eyes filled with tears that streaked down his cheeks.

Now he turned to address the physicals. "There's nothing here. Let's go."

The alarm went silent at the same moment as the digital displays on the incubators went dark. The backup generators were run dry.

Joshua looked at Stanford. "To the desert?" he asked.

"No. Take me to my home."

2.4
HOME

As the van moved through the gateway in the eighty-foot walls, Stanford tried to remember what it was like to cross over the first time, but the feelings failed to materialize. The images in his head were on the opposite side of a dirty lens. Everything was out of focus.

He noticed Joshua staring at him from the front seat.

"They say you died in the shaman's tent," said the mutant.

Stanford met his gaze.

"What did you see when you were dead?"

"I saw the environment."

"You saw inside Salus?"

Stanford nodded.

"What did it look like?"

Stanford noticed other mutants looking at him now, hanging on his every word.

"It was beautiful," he said. "Just like the pictures on the video screens. It's everything you can imagine."

The mutants smiled through the darkness. There was a sense of optimism that percolated inside their damaged bodies.

"But you weren't really there," said Joshua. "It was an illusion."

"I went somewhere," said Stanford. "I saw savanna and prairies and woodlands. I touched a natural waterfall and it felt wet. I went away, but I came back." He looked out the window and heard Joshua's voice rattle against him again.

"Can you get us inside Salus, Mr. Samuels?"

Stanford was quiet for a time, staring out at the tunnel that connected the colonies. The tunnel was blacker than the heavens. He was sure it was the darkest, loneliest place on Ultim.

Finally he looked back at the man and said: "I don't know."

The low hum of the engine was the only sound as the vehicle breached the gateway. The path was unobstructed—the iron fence that had once blocked the tunnel had been left open in haste and indifference. As they passed over the streets of the mutant colony, Stanford looked around for signs of life. There was nothing to see. It was barren here, a virtual ghost town. The place he had once known, he knew no more. These were not the bustling streets of his past. The exodus had been announced for the lucky ones, leaving behind the solitaries and the couplets who had failed to serve the Policy. Curtains were drawn over windows, doors bolted. It was as if the entire colony was holding its collective breath.

When the van touched down in front of Stanford's home, he got out and faced the silent façade. The house itself seemed as though it had been asleep for years. None of the other mutants got out to join him. They knew this was his personal experience. He needed to be alone.

"We'll be back as soon as we round up supplies," said Joshua.

The van whisked off like a nocturnal predator.

Stanford walked up the pathway like he had done a thousand times before, but this time was different. It seemed unnatural, as if some invisible force was propelling him forward and repelling him back at the same time.

He half expected his wife to be waiting on the porch, arms open to embrace him. She would tell him she had a meal waiting on the thermal platter and then ask about his day at the factory. But she was not there. Why would she be?

Stepping onto the stoop, he noticed the front door had been left slightly ajar, perhaps in anticipation of his return. He knew it was not the case. His home was no longer secure. Nothing was what it used to be.

Stanford entered the foyer with caution and immediately swapped his lightweight coat for the panda-hair jacket in the front closet. It was a durable jacket that would keep him warm when the temperature turned harsh. It felt heavy on his shoulders, but not uncomfortable. He was glad it had not been stolen.

Moving through the front hallway he saw the dormant robot aide, right where he had left it. It looked so peaceful there, head slumped, chin resting on a thick metallic chest.

"You were a good friend. I'm glad you had the broca chip. We had good chats. I'm sorry how it turned out."

He patted the robot on the shoulder and continued into the living room. His home was familiar but there was evidence of intrusion. The furniture was out of place by the smallest of margins. When he strode under the archway he saw the cupboards in the kitchen were hanging open, rummaged through by mutants in search of supplies. The violation was not fierce or cruel, but done in a way that suggested an apology. The more time that passed without the suns, the more likely the compassion for fellow man would lessen, and the mutants would turn on each other to fight for their own survival. Like all living things, their natural instincts would compel them to delay their inevitable demise, even though the end would be the same no matter what.

Stanford absent-mindedly attempted to switch on the EM tubes, but they were non-functional. Power had been cut off in the colony, redirected to energy reserves inside Salus.

Removing his sunglasses, he cast the rays of his glowing eyes upon the old boy's food dish on the floor near the refrigerator. He could see the dish was still half full. The burglars had stripped the kitchen entirely of food, but left kibble for the missing dog.

He approached the table and sat heavily in his dining chair. He imagined Sarah sitting opposite, staring back with her chestnut eyes. He smiled back at the empty seat and felt a tightening in his chest. He was barely holding on.

Out of the corner of his eye he thought he saw the old boy scampering through the archway, but when he shot his head around there was nothing there. Memories were fluttering back like moths to the porch light.

Poor old boy, he thought. *I hope you're okay.*

He felt overwhelmed by guilt. He put his head in his hands and wept.

I'm sorry. I'm so sorry. I failed the Policy. I failed my family.

He stayed like that for a long time before finally making his way down the hallway to the bedroom. He could see his breath condensing in the crisp darkness as he pressed the buttons on the dual sleep transmitters. They crackled and fizzled before shorting out. Everything was dying. He collapsed on the bed and covered himself over with blankets.

Turning his eye-beams toward the bathroom, he saw the toilet where his wife had sat with the pregnancy monitor, her broken body almost completely drained of hope. He remembered her trembling hands, the fear in her eyes. She provided the dominant gene that brought them together. He wept for her now. All she wanted was a child.

I'm so sorry, my darling. I have to leave you now. I came back to see if you were waiting, but I know you are gone. I am heartbroken. If I could do anything to change things and bring you back, I would. I love you, Sarah. But this is the last time I will come to this house. You are the love of my life, but I must go.

After a while he felt his strength return enough to lift off the bed and walk back to the foyer. He brushed by the robot aide and, for an instant, considered pressing the power button, just so he could have one last conversation and say goodbye.

"Goodbye, old friend."

Stanford patted the inert robot on the shoulder and glanced at his wife's portrait on the wall.

"I love you, Sarah . . . you will be forever in my dreams."

A single tear brimmed over his wife's eye and streaked down the picture frame.

Stanford's heart ached as he exited his home on the walkway. The pain was different than the physical pain he had experienced from the I-132. The pain of saying goodbye was much worse.

He knew this was the last time he would be in his home, the last time he would be in the mutant colony. Everything he knew was gone. Now the only direction was forward—toward the dome of Salus.

The van, back from scavenging, lay in wait.

He felt the rings of Saturn overflowing with tears.

2.5
CHECK IN

Atoms crackled beneath the passenger seats as the fusion train cruised across the grassy plains of Salus' eastern sector. To the north, the Perfect subdivision had already been filled out; rows upon rows of opulent houses cut into the sides of the fertile rolling hills.

A beautiful emerald lake was surrounded by majestic pine trees, with multiple green spaces and a view of snow-capped mountains on the distant horizon. Houses in the nearby neighborhood were arranged in square blocks, smaller than the houses to the north, all two stories with fenced-in yards and well manicured lawns. The sector exuded an aura of comfort and community.

When the train settled in the terminal, the doors shot open, spilling thousands of mutants and Eradicators onto the platform. The passengers were immediately directed to the assembly stations by overhead loudspeakers.

"Please approach your assigned kiosk to obtain the ticket to your home in the immaculate new environment. You will not be permitted into the sector until you have received your residential number. Once you and your couplet have been cleared, feel free to wander the surroundings and enjoy all the amenities Salus has to offer. To avoid congestion in the terminal, we encourage you to refrain from searching for your offspring until after you have gained access to the residential community.

"Welcome to the eastern subdivision. We hope you enjoy your new life . . ."

A woman with a floppy suns hat and brightly colored eye makeup clutched her husband's hand as they crossed the platform. She craned her neck to scan the crowd.

"I don't see Michael," she said.

"They told us to wait," said her husband. "We need to check in."

"He must be here." Her eyes grew wide and trembled. "William, he must be here. Tell me he must."

"Of course he's here, Audrey. I'm sure they'll have information at the kiosks. You need to calm down. It's not healthy for you to work yourself up like this. This is what we've prepared for."

Audrey burst into a sudden fit of laughter. "Of course you're right! I know it. Michael is here. A mother knows."

They held tightly to one another as they navigated through the dense crowd to the nearest kiosk.

The husband smiled. "Let's check in," he said.

"It's simply gorgeous here," said Audrey. "Did you see how green that lake was? It was like a perfect sheet of beveled glass."

"Yes, darling, it's beautiful. Everything is beautiful here. Are you surprised? This is exactly what they told us it would be."

The woman threw her hands in the air with overzealous excitement. "You'll be able to take Michael fishing. He'll love that. I will cook the fish and serve it for dinner. Won't that be wonderful?"

Her husband nodded. "Yes, and I'll take Michael hunting in the wooded region. I'll show him how to skin a deer."

Audrey furrowed her thinly plucked eyebrows. "You've never skinned a deer, William. How do you know the first thing about skinning a deer?"

"How hard can it be? There are tutorials on the video screen."

"Why would you want to skin a deer in the first place?" She peered at her husband from beneath the brim of her hat. "I don't want little Michael skinning a deer. Promise me you won't do that."

The man chuckled and squeezed his wife's hand. "I promise. I didn't realize you felt so strongly about it. We'll stick to fishing."

"Okay, I don't mind skinning a fish."

"How is skinning a fish different than skinning a deer?"

"Well, a deer is a larger animal, William. That's how."

"What does size have to do with it? They are both living creatures. This is Salus, darling. The animals are genuine."

"Living in the sea is different than living on the land."

"How so?"

"It just is. Now stop pestering me, William. You can skin a fish. I give you permission."

"Technically, dear, you don't skin a fish. You fillet a fish. It's all about technique. You don't want to choke on a bone."

Audrey scrunched her nose. "You delight in torturing me, William. You know it's not good to be stressed in my condition."

The man laughed and leaned close to kiss her on the cheek. "I'm sorry," he said, rubbing his hand affectionately along the enlarged belly of her wrap-around dress.

They had arrived at the front of the line. The kiosk attendant peered inquisitively at the couple and then glanced down at a portable data terminal. "What's your coupling registration number?" he asked.

"We are Audrey and William Hampton, registration number 22565."

The attendant inputted the number into the terminal. After a short delay, he regarded William. "You are the mutant?"

"Yes."

"I need a sample, Mr. Hampton."

William looked at his wife, and then back at the attendant. "Yes, of course."

The attendant beckoned an on-site medic.

A medic in white scrubs stepped forward and produced a thumb-sized thermal cylinder. "Kindly stick out your tongue."

William complied, and within seconds his tongue had been swabbed and the genetic sample inputted in the cylinder.

"Your father was an alcoholic," said the medic, analyzing the data immediately.

"Yes."

"And you were genetically predisposed to alcoholism."

William nodded. "The gene was eradicated." He smiled at his wife.

The medic's head was bent toward the terminal.

William pulled his wife tightly to his side. "I am very lucky to have such a beautiful Eradicator. And I'm very much looking forward to being reunited with my son. There are four of us now, with Michael and another on the way."

The medic looked between the man and wife. "Have a good day."

The attendant handed a ticket across the kiosk. "Your home is in the northeast quadrant. You have a beautiful view of the mountains from your living room window. The snow is there year-round. I hope you find it pleasant."

"Thank you," said William. "I'm sure we will."

Audrey squeezed her husband's hand as she addressed the attendant. "When will we be reunited with our son?"

The attendant stared at her with a blank expression. "I have no idea," he said. "Good luck to you."

"What do you mean?" asked Audrey.

The attendant looked past her to the next couple in line. "Next couplet, step forward," he said.

"I asked you a question about Michael," said Audrey, her voice cracking now.

William pulled his wife by the arm. "Honey, let's go home."

"Home?"

"Yes," he said. "Our new home."

Audrey looked into her husband's eyes and felt a sense of calm instantly wash over her. "Okay, William," she said. "Take me home. Oh, I'm just dying to see what the baby's room looks like. It will have a room for the baby, won't it?"

"Of course it will. The house is fully prepared."

They walked arm in arm toward the exit, passing hundreds of couplets awaiting tickets to their new lives in the immaculate neighborhoods.

"I can't believe you would skin a deer," said Audrey.

William chuckled.

"Promise me you won't do such a thing. I don't want our children exposed to such savagery."

"I promise."

"I think Michael will like fishing. The lake is so spectacular. Like a sheet of green glass."

2.6
CLEANSING

The van lurked silently through the black streets of the mutant colony. The residents who had not served the Policy were on a death sentence. Perhaps it was pride that kept them indoors. Even in the face of death, pride was worth preserving. This place had always been a colony of tortured people, but the torture was never more evident than now. Everything seemed worse in the dark.

Stanford fought the urge to think about his home as the vehicle left the city limits. He had gone back to achieve a sense of closure, but there was no closing a lifetime of memories. The more he fought it, the more he thought about his wife, about the old boy, about his son.

The harder he tried to shut out the past, the more it forced its way in. There was no deadbolt on his mind.

As tears welled in his eyes, he felt a hand on his shoulder and turned to see the face of the resident mother, Janice. She smiled warmly.

"Why do you carry so much pain?" she asked. Her voice was soothing.

Stanford's voice cracked. "I miss my family."

"Of course you do. We all do."

"I can't do it, Mother. I'm not the person you think I am. I can't meet your expectations."

The mother smiled. "Mr. Samuels, what you are going through is exactly what we all went through. The only difference is that we've had years in the desert to pick ourselves back up. How long have you had?"

Stanford noticed how warm her eyes were amidst her rotting flesh. He felt comforted. There was hope inside the agony.

"All you need to do is to release some of your pain," she said. "You need to rid it from your soul and never see it return."

"How do I do that?"

"We can do it right now. All we need is a campfire. I have something that can help you."

"What is it?"

The mother's smile never faded.

He felt safe in her presence.

"I'll take care of you, Mr. Samuels. When I'm done, you'll retain the memories but the pain will be gone."

Stanford nodded. He had seen the way she took care of the android's baby. She was maternal, and he desperately needed a mother's touch.

Janice called forward to the driver. "Stop at the boundary. We have something we need to do."

Stanford felt the thrusters shift beneath him as the vehicle veered off the main road, settling at a dead end a few miles from the shadow of the great wall. Looking out the rear window, the skyline of the mutant colony was dark and silent.

"Don't worry," said Janice. "It will be okay."

The side door slid open and the mother led Stanford out by the hand. Joshua and Jack fetched some kindling from the trunk and started a small fire off the side of the road in the sand. The other mutants gathered around to warm their cold appendages while the mother set a clay pot of water on the fire with a feathery fern frond steeping inside.

"What is it?" asked Stanford, taking a seat near the fire. The scent of the bubbling stew reached his nostrils.

Janice smiled. "It will help you feel better."

Stanford felt momentarily lightheaded. He tensed as he saw the face of the Director staring back from across the fire.

He shuffled away. The face of the Director vanished. "I'm sorry," he said. "I can't do this."

"Sure you can," said Janice. "What you are feeling is perfectly natural. It is all part of the process. This will help."

Stanford's mind flashed with the image of the Director's body plastered to the front of the military vehicle, chest ripped open to expose circuits and wires. Graphic hallucinations were revealing themselves from his subconscious.

He stood up. "I appreciate your help, but let's just get in the van and continue on." His head was swirling.

Without warning, Stanford was restrained by strong arms gripping him from behind. The presence overpowered him, and before he had time to react, he was taken to the ground.

The resident mother stood over him.

"Open his mouth," she demanded.

Stanford clenched his jaw as tightly as he could, but the rotting fingers of his captors pried his teeth apart, allowing the mother to pour the steeped tea down the back of his throat. The liquid burned and he began to choke. The harder he tried to gasp for air the more he felt himself drowning.

Through blurred vision he saw the demonic eyes of the physicals standing over him. Brilliant fires of crimson and ash exploded in the night sky.

And then there was only blackness . . .

2.7
HEALING

Dipping his legs in the shallow pool, the phosphorescence appeared like glittering green algae whenever he made a churning motion. The continuous sound of the waterfall put Stanford at ease. He felt completely comfortable seated on the bank.

He looked up and saw clear blue sky, two brilliant suns at their zeniths. There was no dome here. He watched a collection of geese overhead as they formed a migration pattern and disappeared on the horizon. Stanford could hear the sound of their calls long after they vanished from sight. This was the sound of freedom, he thought, and when he sniffed the fresh air, he realized he had never felt so free of burden. It was as if his pain had dissipated into the cloudless heavens.

When he looked down at his legs, he saw the face of his child floating up between his knees. The lips were blue, the skin pale and swollen. He jumped up with a start and noticed the image had vanished. There was only calm blue water.

From behind he heard the voice of the assassin: "Mr. Samuels, why do we have to keep meeting like this?"

Stanford spun around to see the assassin making his way through the clearing.

"I come in peace, Stanford. I assume you are unarmed?"

Stanford nodded.

"Do you know why you are here?" he asked.

Stanford looked around at the scenery and then back at the scarred face of the assassin. "No."

"You drank the fern, Stanford. You've been transported to a place of healing. The process can sometimes have strange side effects. Have you seen anything unusual?"

Directly behind the assassin, moving through the dense underbrush, Stanford saw a procession of naked women with dark, shoulder-length hair and metallic breasts disappearing into the vegetation.

"I don't feel well. My mind is jumbled."

"You are in an induced coma, Stanford. It's the only way to rid your pain. The fern can make your memories more palatable. It will adjust things slightly to make everything better."

"How do you know what's better?"

Stanford was suddenly transported to a field of a million ferns. There were no signs of civilization in any direction. He was standing knee-deep in a sea of feathery fronds. He looked to his right and saw the assassin approaching.

"How did you do that?"

The assassin smiled.

"I've been here before," said Stanford, looking around.

"Of course you have. You were born to be our leader. Everything that will happen is already in your mind, both the good and the bad. The fern puts things into focus. We are all a construct of your imagination, Stanford. You determine the course of things."

Stanford picked a healthy leaf and sniffed its aroma. "It's organic."

"When the Patron dropped the bombs and banished us to the desert, we noticed ferns starting to sprout out of the ash. They thrived. We couldn't harvest them fast enough. We were short on food and so we ate the plants. They resisted at first, as if they were defending themselves. We couldn't chew through them, couldn't break the outer skin. But for whatever reason, they gave in. That's when we noticed their unique properties. They are a gift."

"They're medicinal?"

"Yes. And that's why we have an advantage, Stanford. The Patron blew us out of the sky thirty years ago, and he thinks we are sitting in the desert licking our wounds. He has no idea what power we can unleash on him. We've spent three decades getting healthy, raiding the colonies for ammunition. We are ready for him now. This is the start of the real revolution. What you've seen so far is nothing. We haven't even touched our true potential."

Stanford dropped the fern frond. "And what do you want from me?"

"Stanford, there is so much for you to accomplish. You are held back by your past. Your pain is crippling. The only thing to do is to start fresh. How did you feel when you saw Sarah back there in the forest?"

"Was Sarah there?"

Out of the corner of his eye, Stanford caught a glimpse of the old boy running through a thick patch of ferns. He made a move to follow.

"Wait," said the assassin. "Don't go."

Stanford looked back at the assassin. "I need to go to him. He could show me to my child."

"Your child is in Salus. You must stay with us to get to him."

"You don't know that."

"Yes, I do. And you do, too. That's why I am in your imagination. You chose me to be your messenger."

"I must make amends with my dog. I abandoned him."

The assassin stood in his way. "There is only one way to make up for your past regrets."

"Tell me."

The assassin grabbed Stanford around the throat and took him to the ground with a single, expert movement. "This is the way to make amends, Mr. Samuels. This is the only way."

Stanford locked his jaw but the assassin pressed his nostrils until he was forced to gasp for breath. With Stanford sucking oxygen, the assassin took the opportunity to stuff a fern frond into the back of his throat. The frond expanded when it came in contact with saliva and began to choke off Stanford's oxygen supply.

"I'm killing your sorrow," said the assassin. "Don't fight it."

Stanford clutched his throat. His face went deep blue.

"Let it happen, Stanford. It will all be over in a moment."

Stanford flipped onto his hands and knees and vomited a puddle of green liquid onto the ashen soil. The liquid pooled and began to harden like candle wax. From it, a new fern began to sprout.

Stanford strained to breathe. He reached into his mouth and pulled out a fern frond the size of his forearm before collapsing on his back once again.

The assassin stood over him. "You're evacuated. The healing is done."

2.8
REBIRTH REDUX

A galaxy of stars was in Stanford's eyes when he woke up supine on the side of the road. He heard the sound of movement to his left and craned his neck to see the physicals climbing back into the vehicle. His first instinct was to stay there and let the van drive off; to go back to the waterfall inside his own head where he could find Sarah and the old boy and be at peace, but the voice of the resident mother brought him back.

"How are you feeling?" she asked. She sat down next to him in the sand and cradled his head in her arms.

Stanford glanced into her eyes. She seemed like an angel to him. "I don't feel anything," he said. His voice was weak.

"Do you know where you are?"

He looked across at the smoldering fire. "We're at the boundary. We're going to look for my son."

"And what else?"

"We're going to take Salus by force. We need to get back to the camp."

The mother smiled. "Do you know why you are laying here?"

"No." His throat was sore.

"It's time to go."

The mother helped him to his feet. He clutched his stomach as he stood upright and held onto the mother for support until the dizziness passed.

Moments later, he was inside the van as it plunged into a pit in the ground, following a subterranean passage beneath the great wall.

Slumped in a window seat, Stanford's body felt heavy, his mind groggy.

Joshua moved to the seat next to him. "You look like you could use some water."

Stanford flinched.

"Take it easy." Joshua handed over a small ceramic cup.

Stanford sniffed the contents and then swallowed it down with one gulp.

"Slow down, Mr. Samuels. We don't want that coming back up." He patted Stanford on the knee. "I have a few questions."

"It hurts to talk."

Joshua passed the cup into the forward cabin. "Get Mr. Samuels some more water." He turned his attention back to Stanford. "This won't take long. Some of my questions may seem strange, but just answer as best as you can."

"What did you do to me?"

"Be patient, Mr. Samuels. I must follow protocol."

Stanford stared out at the dark cavern as Joshua's voice continued.

"You spoke of your wife while you were out. Was she in your dream?"

Stanford hesitated. "There were women. They weren't human."

"What happened to your wife, Mr. Samuels?"

"I don't know. I thought they changed her into a machine, but I don't know."

"So one of the women in your dream could have been her?"

Stanford paused to look at the man.

"I know this is hard, Mr. Samuels. The aim of the questions is to determine if you've been cleansed. It will be over in a moment."

Stanford's head felt thick. "Cleansed?"

"Stay with me. Do you yearn for your wife, Mr. Samuels?"

Stanford was silent for a time. "I thought I did . . ."

"But you don't now?"

He faltered, confused by his lack of feeling.

Joshua continued. "You talked about a dog. He was there with you."

"Yes."

"What's his name?"

"He has no name."

"You wanted to follow him somewhere. Where did he go?"

Stanford thought about it. "I abandoned him."

"Do you regret that?"

There was nothing inside him. He was an empty shell.

"Mr. Samuels, you've consumed a large dose of the fern. It will take time for your mind and body to readjust. This is how it should be."

"Did you poison me?"

"No, we didn't poison you. We anesthetized your past. The fern accelerated the grieving process by numbing your pain. I'm sorry if you feel betrayed, but it's best for us, and it's best for you. If you want to find your son, you need to leave everything else behind. There's no time to dwell on what happened before now. You wanted to walk forward, now you can. We just gave you a little boost." He handed Stanford the ceramic cup. "I have one more question. Then we're done."

Stanford took a long sip and stared through his double-tinted sunglasses. He felt the copper in his irises cooling like embers on a dying fire.

"We've received intel about a compound in the outer boundaries, about thirty miles from Salus. We don't know what's happening inside, but we know androids have been spotted. There are helix dogs."

Stanford passed the cup back to Joshua before removing his sunglasses. The copper flecks in his irises were stationary; the rays no longer shone.

Joshua stared back. "Your eyes are normal."

Stanford barely recognized his own reflection in the side window. He looked back at the man. "Will my feelings return?"

"You are still capable of feeling in the here and now. Your memories will stay with you—some may take time to fully crystallize—but you will have no emotional reaction to anything prior to this moment."

"Is it permanent?"

"For some it lasts for years. Others never get it back."

"I'm no better than an android."

"Keep your son in mind, Mr. Samuels."

Stanford squeezed his eyelids together and tried to picture Sarah's face, but her image failed to materialize. The memory of his son in the incubator was out of focus. He could not tap into his past. Anything that might evoke an emotional response in his brain was blocked by the chemicals he'd ingested from the fern.

He opened his eyes and saw that the vehicle had returned to the surface. The engine hummed along the desert landscape in the outer boundaries.

"Do you feel up to this, Mr. Samuels?"

He looked at Joshua. "Let's go to the compound," he said.

"Are you sure?"

"I have nothing left back there. Let's go."

Joshua addressed the mutant in the driver's seat. "You heard him. Let's go."

The van's headlights extinguished at the same time as rear thrusters ignited in the undercarriage, sending the vehicle like a dart into the darkness.

Stanford clutched the armrest, staring straight ahead. He knew he should feel anger toward the physicals who had stolen his ability to emotionally connect to his past, but he was incapable of conjuring anger, or sadness, or anything else that had happened before now. They had taken that from him, and he had no way of knowing if he'd ever get it back. The worst part was that he didn't know if it was good or bad. He no longer had a frame of reference, nothing to compare. He had been reset to zero. All he felt at this moment was emptiness, as if his nerve-endings had been cauterized by scorching flames. There was a small distinction between humans and androids—a gap that was closing with each passing moment—and Stanford couldn't help but think he was closer to a machine than a man.

Maybe it's for the best, he thought.

Joshua's voice invaded his mind.

"We use sonar to reduce potential detection. We won't crash, Mr. Samuels. Don't worry."

Stanford could feel the tug of the g-force as the van snaked through the silent dunes. Glancing into the back seat, he could barely make out the figure of the resident mother. He desperately needed to see her warm smile. He needed her to jumpstart his own humanity.

Sensing his vulnerability, she spoke through the darkness. "You are strong, Mr. Samuels. Don't begrudge us for this. It is the only way to go forward. You will see."

Her words slowly filled his empty soul. The swirling in his stomach ceased, his head was clear. He felt entirely at ease.

He heard the mother's voice again. "The fern has eliminated your agony."

Stanford spoke quietly. "I know I should feel guilty for leaving my people behind, but I don't."

"There's no time for guilt, Mr. Samuels. The fern has made sure you won't feel it again. If Salus is to be breached, you need to be focused on one goal. This is how it must be."

Stanford watched her shadowy figure. "I feel inhuman."

"Mr. Samuels, you are still very much a functioning human, I promise."

"Is this what happened to you?"

"We all react differently to the fern. It seems to recognize what we need most, and it amplifies or dulls those emotions within us, as the case may be. My past is what drives me. For you, it worked the opposite way, but you must trust that it's the best way."

"What about them?" he asked, referring to the physicals.

Janice smiled. "The fern gave us all another chance, Mr. Samuels."

Stanford thought for a moment before the radio crackled on the console. He turned to the front to see Joshua pick up the receiver. A voice Stanford recognized came over the radio waves.

"What's your twenty, Joshua?"

The voice belonged to the assassin.

Joshua spoke into the receiver. "We'll be at the target compound in T-minus five minutes."

The voice came back. "This is a reconnaissance mission, Joshua. I don't want any aggressive action taken without the whole team present. The base is high risk."

"I read you, Mr. Dekkar."

"How is Mr. Samuels?"

"He's recovering."

"Put him on."

Joshua handed over the receiver and changed places with Stanford.

The assassin's voice crackled through the poor reception. "Mr. Samuels, how are you feeling?"

Stanford took a peek through the windshield. There was only blackness. "I don't feel," he said.

"I understand. I'm glad to have you aboard, Stanford. We need each other. I know this is hard."

There was a pause.

"Listen, Stanford, we need you back at the base. You could really give our morale a boost. Don't stay out there too long, okay?"

Stanford took a moment. "We'll be back before the suns rise."

The assassin chuckled. "Your sense of humor is still intact, Mr. Samuels. Just be careful out there. Get back as soon as you can. There's a lot we need to discuss."

The line went dead.

Stanford retook his seat next to Joshua as the van hummed across the dunes.

"This will be your first mission as a Tech Terrorist. There's a lot expected of you, Mr. Samuels. You heard Mr. Dekkar. Morale is low. The mutants at the base expect more than a soldier."

"They might be disappointed," returned Stanford.

"All we need is hope, Mr. Samuels."

Stanford glanced around at each of the physicals, feeling their eyes burrowing into him. He could hear their pleas for help in his mind, like a recurring nightmare. Thirty years of suffering had fallen on his shoulders. He suddenly realized that he had exchanged his personal pain for the pain of thousands.

As he took in the images of the grotesque creatures, he felt his seat shift beneath him. The passengers instinctively gripped the armrests.

Without warning, the vehicle veered sharply, sending the mutants careening into the side walls.

"What's going on?" screamed Joshua.

"I'm not sure," said the driver.

The thrusters brought the van to a sudden stop, once again jostling the passengers in their seats.

The driver looked at Joshua with wide eyes. "The sonar must have picked up something at the last minute."

"So turn on the headlights," yelled Joshua.

The driver quickly ignited the vehicle's lamps, illuminating the stretch of barren desert before them.

"There's nothing there, sir."

The mutant battalion stared intently through the windshield at a cloud of dust and nuclear ash churned up by the thrusters. By all appearances, the passengers were utterly alone in Ultim's most desolate region.

The interior of the van was silent. Stanford could see his breath condensing in the crisp air.

Joshua finally spoke. "Recalculate the sonar, Jack. Let's get back on course."

The driver adjusted the controls on the console.

"The desert has a way of confusing the sonar, Mr. Samuels." Joshua looked out the windshield for obstructions as the vehicle continued forward. "There's nothing but empty space out here. A lot of times it's a dust cloud that throws things off track." He turned to address the crew. "Be vigilant, mutants."

The driver suddenly pointed out the windshield. "There's something there!"

At the very distant range of the headlights, something scooted across the sand on all fours.

"What is it?" asked Joshua.

Stanford shifted in his seat to get a better look.

Whatever had been there was not there now.

"I'm not sure," said the driver. "It looked like an animal of some kind."

"That's probably what it was," said Joshua. "What's the reading on the sonar?"

"Recalculation is complete. We're T-minus 2 minutes, sir; 140 degrees due west."

Joshua peered out at the darkness. "Let's take it by foot. Load up. Don't forget the infrareds."

"Is it a good idea to go out there?" asked Stanford, feeling a sudden wave of panic.

Joshua looked directly into Stanford's dormant eyes. "We're the Tech Terrorists, Mr. Samuels. You are one of us now. Get out of the van and lead your men."

The mutants were outside in moments.

Before leaving the vehicle, Stanford looked back at the figure of the resident mother.

"Good luck," she said.

Stanford nodded and exited the side door. He felt his breathing getting rapid. As soon as his feet hit the sand, Joshua spoke.

"Mutants, this mission will be led by Mr. Stanford Samuels. He gives the orders. Listen to him, fight for him, and protect him like you would each other. Do you understand?"

The mutants responded in unison. "Yes, sir!"

Joshua handed Stanford an oxygen mask. "Put this on. You don't want the toxic dust in your lungs. It chokes off your airway in a hurry."

Stanford took a few steps forward and looked back at the assembled men. They stopped when he stopped, and advanced when he did. They had accepted him as their leader, and they all moved as a single entity.

Stanford felt more powerful than he had ever felt in his life. Everything that had happened up to that point—the pain and the sorrow and the suffering—culminated in a single moment of truth; and in that single moment he was a king.

He was no longer the man with Wilson's disease from the mutant colony. That man was gone now, left behind with his former life. He would remember it—he would remember Sarah, and the old boy, and the Iron Man, and Ilsa K—but he would no longer be crippled by guilt and regret. The weight had been lifted, anesthetized by the fern. This was his new life, free of burden.

He felt the copper swirling in his irises again. The beams returned to his eyes, lighting a path on the sand. He stopped his advance and took a deep breath, feeling a sense of calm wash through his entire body. Once he was relaxed, the beams dimmed.

He looked back at the mutant soldiers. They watched him closely, waiting for direction. Stanford stared forward into the darkness. As an experiment, he squeezed his palms into tight fists and tensed his arms and shoulders. He clenched his jaw, feeling the strain through his limbs like vibrations. The fire reignited in his eyes, illuminating the sand once again.

From behind he heard the voice of Joshua.

"Mr. Samuels, what are we waiting for?"

Stanford looked back. "I can control it," he said.

Joshua approached quickly. "You can control what?"

"I can control my eyes."

"Stanford, are you okay to proceed?"

Stanford dimmed his eyes automatically. For the first time since his mutation had exacerbated, he could control the flow of light.

"You've gone through a lot, Stanford. Are you sure you're up for this? I know I've been hard on you. I can take over until you are ready."

Stanford put his hand on Joshua's shoulder. "There's only one way to find out if I'm ready."

Joshua nodded and stepped back, watching Stanford advance through the night, cutting the darkness with the high beams from his eyes. The footfalls of the men stirred up the terrain. The oxygen mask protected Stanford's lungs from airborne particles of nuclear ash.

Within minutes, the outline of a rectangular building was visible a few hundred yards due west. The squadron assembled behind the shelter of a sand dune.

Joshua knelt down beside Stanford and handed him the binoculars.

Stanford turned his eye-beams off and stared through the infrared lenses. He had a clear view of the compound. The only sign of life was a ferocious-looking helix dog patrolling the entrance.

"What do you see?" asked Joshua.

Stanford looked a moment longer before setting down the binoculars. "There's a dog."

"What else?"

"Nothing else."

Joshua exhaled deeply. "We'll have to get inside. If intel reports androids, then we can be sure they're in there."

"This is a reconnaissance mission," said Stanford. "We will discuss it as a team back at the camp."

"It's a small compound, Mr. Samuels. We have enough firepower to get in and out in a few minutes. Let's annihilate the synthetics before they know what hit them. Then we can concentrate on Salus."

"Salus is always the goal, Joshua, but you heard Mr. Dekkar's orders. We'll make a plan back at the base. I'm in charge and it's my decision to retreat."

Joshua smirked. "The power went straight to your head, Mr. Samuels." He turned to address the mutants. "You heard him. Get back to the van."

Before leaving the dune, Stanford took one last glance through the binoculars. He watched the helix dog pacing back and forth until it stopped suddenly and hunched its back in attack mode. It began to snarl and bark at the darkness before whimpering and cowering from an invisible threat.

Stanford scanned to the left with the binoculars, and saw what appeared to be a pack of animals scampering on all fours across the sand. They were headed right in his direction, and moving fast. As they got nearer, Stanford saw that they weren't animals at all, but naked human children. They bared teeth and howled like wild beasts.

Stanford turned to the soldiers. The copper in his irises was swirling like hellfire. "Back to the van. Now!"

The mutants retreated across the uneven terrain as fast as they could. Several of them tripped in the dunes but managed to pick themselves back up quickly. Sounds of howling filled the night sky.

Stanford was nearly out of breath; his legs were about to give out. The van was within sight.

Joshua grabbed him by the shoulder of his panda jacket and propelled him forward for the final stretch.

When they arrived at the van, the resident mother slid open the side door, and the mutants jumped inside and bolted the locks.

The driver switched on the headlights.

In front of the van was the pack of wild children. They were young, no more than five or six years old. They walked on all fours, growling and snarling like wolves. They communicated through grunts and whimpers. The pack wandered around the perimeter of the van, sniffing the exterior and bumping into it with their bodies. Several of the children jumped on the hood while others began rocking the vehicle back and forth. They pulled at the door handles.

"Get us out of here," shouted Joshua.

"No," said Stanford. "If we move we may injure one of them."

"Who cares if we injure one of them?" yelled Joshua. "They're animals."

Stanford's eyes shone with intensity. He cast his spotlights directly on Joshua. "They are human children. We won't harm them."

Joshua shielded his eyes.

The van rocked back and forth and then suddenly the children assembled at the front of the vehicle and ran off together into the darkness. The sound of howling slowly faded away.

The interior of the van was dead silent for a long moment.

Stanford looked back at the resident mother. She was expressionless.

The driver finally spoke. "Can we get out of here?"

Stanford's eyes dimmed. He looked around the van at the dark figures.

The engine ignited in the undercarriage and the van lifted off the sand and sped through the night.

2.9
THE BASE

The rebel base in the desert was only a few miles from Salus. From their vantage, the dome appeared to be almost entirely consumed by savage ferns. Only the crown was visible through the rich foliage.

When the van arrived, Stanford stepped out and followed Joshua across the sand to the main tent. Entering through the flap, he dimmed his eyes and saw a man seated near a campfire.

The man turned to face him. "Stanford Samuels. It's nice to see you again."

Fresh pustules festered on the assassin's chin.

"It's nice to see you too, Markus."

The assassin smiled and looked toward the tent door at his second in command. "I presume Joshua was an adequate guide. Thank you, Joshua. You can leave us now."

Joshua nodded and exited the tent.

When he was gone, the assassin gestured for Stanford to join him by the fire. "Were you able to accomplish your goal in the mutant colony, Mr. Samuels?"

"You made sure of it." Stanford stood by the edge of the fire.

"I suppose I did," said the assassin. "Sit down and

61

warm yourself. It's getting colder out there by the minute. Who knows how much longer we have."

As he crouched, Stanford noticed the body of the shaman on a cot at the far end of the tent.

"He's in a coma, Stanford. The shaman is not well. I'm medicating him with the fern every few hours, but it's not looking good."

"What happened?"

"Old age happened. The shaman is the eldest statesman of the Tech Terrorists. He's been through two wars. He's the only physical to ever encounter the Patron face to face. His body is beaten and tired. Time catches up to all of us eventually."

"When did he meet the Patron?"

"He was detained in the first war. The story goes that he was captured in the colony and tortured for three weeks before being cast into the outer boundaries. He was a virtual skeleton when he took shelter in the dunes. Lord knows why they chose to release him. Perhaps they knew releasing him was a fate worse than death. His body was badly beaten, but he never spoke a single word to the Patron. It's amazing he survived. Nobody can verify the story, and the shaman never speaks of it. You know how legends tend to grow. But I don't doubt a word of it. He was an incredibly strong man and still is, but the end is coming. The mutants need a new leader, Mr. Samuels."

Stanford watched the shaman's chest slowly rise and fall.

"I know how difficult this is for you, Stanford. We've all lost families and had our lives changed forever. We've all suffered in ways that human beings are not meant to suffer. We keep memories that haunt us in the night."

"You stole my memories."

"We stole your pain. Your memories are not compromised."

"I can't remember what it felt like the first time I saw my son. You had no right to take that from me."

The assassin absently poked at the fire with a stick. "You're right. I can't pretend to know what it's like to have a wife and a son, but that doesn't mean that I—or any of us—suffer any more or any less. The Patron stole from us. Loss is loss, no matter how much or how many. It hurts just the same. I may not have been a father, but I had parents who were sacrificed in the name of the Policy—"

He went quiet, poking at the fire.

Stanford turned his head toward the shaman. The man was gaunt and pale, the skin hung from his arms like bags of worn leather. This is what had become of the man of legends. There was no magic fern concoction that could reverse the hands of time.

He looked across the fire at the assassin. "How did you lose your parents?"

The assassin took a moment. "I wasn't born like this. I was normal once, as normal as any other little boy with a mutated TREM2 gene. I was an only child with two strong, honest parents. They owned a small grocery store in the central sector. They sold fresh produce before the farmland was contaminated. I used to love when my father took me to work with him. He let me stock the shelves and press the buttons on the digital register. My mother was already suffering from early onset Alzheimer's. She did the books and handled a lot of the inventory. She wasn't as comfortable as my father with the public due to her condition, which was accelerating relatively quickly, but she could handle it in a pinch. My parents were brave people. They provided for me, and no matter how difficult life was for them, they made sure I was instilled with the right moral code . . ."

The assassin trailed off.

Stanford stared at the campfire.

"I never saw or heard from my father after he was conscripted," said the assassin. "It wasn't long after he was gone that my mother's condition worsened. She held on as long as she could, but she was losing the battle. I remember sitting at the foot of her bed, telling her that she could let go . . . that I'd be okay. I hated seeing her like that, and I promised that I'd fight for her so she would no longer have to. I'll always remember how she smiled and squeezed my hand, as if she could understand what I was saying even though the disease had stolen her words."

The assassin paused to poke at the fire.

"I'm sorry," said Stanford.

The assassin seemed not to hear him.

"After she passed," he continued, "I was sent to a home for mutant orphans. There were lots of them sprouting up in the colonies as more and more families were ripped apart. The place was run by antiquated robot aides that barely functioned. That's where I learned most of my combat skills. If you couldn't stand your ground, you didn't eat. The children were cruel. If you think the Tech Terrorists are savages, you haven't seen anything. It was anarchy inside that place. I think the Patron wanted it that way. It wasn't enough that we had lost our parents, he wanted to punish us for being mutants, as if we asked to be born imperfect. But I suppose I should thank him for helping me fulfill my promise to my mother. He made sure I had the skills to fight for her memory."

"How old were you?"

"I was nine when I went in. Most of the residents were anywhere from eight to fifteen. I remember an older boy named Clint something. I forget his last name. I haven't seen him since. He's the one who told me about the Tech Terrorists. His uncle had recently joined the secret opposition party. Clint got me interested and told me stories about the underground tunnels. I decided that if the Patron could take my father away from his son and dying wife, I wanted nothing to do with him. I certainly wouldn't fight for him. Clint gave me connections and helped me and another boy get to the secret cell in the mutant colony. The other boy was Joshua. We've been with the rebels ever since. The time I spent in the home obliterated the moral code my parents worked so hard to instill in me. It changed me into the person I am today. This is me, Stanford. Like me or hate me. But I think they would approve." The assassin looked up from the fire, meeting Stanford's eyes. "What happened to your folks, Stanford? Were they conscripted?"

"My father was in charge of shipping artillery to the front lines. It's because of his job that he and my mother avoided conscription."

"How did they die?"

Stanford shook his head. "There's no use talking about it. I can't remember what it felt like to lose them. I feel empty."

"The fern treatment was necessary, Stanford. I wouldn't have ordered it had I thought there was another way. But you were shackled to your past. Your memories would have consumed you eventually. You wouldn't have been able to fulfill your mission. We did this for you as much as we did it for us. You will need all your faculties if you want to find your boy."

"Why don't you do it to your own people? They seem to be suffering plenty."

"A deep cleansing is rare. We needed to get right into your core. Your suffering was your crutch. The physicals are defined by their pain—it's the engine that propels us."

Stanford felt his eyes growing hot. He cast beams of light upon the shaman.

"What's happening to your eyes, Stanford?"

"I can control them now."

"Show me."

Stanford took a deep breath and slowly exhaled until his lungs felt like empty sacks in his chest. He closed his eyes and allowed his muscles to relax; his arms hung at his sides like limp ropes. When he opened his eyes again, the copper in his irises was calm and dormant.

The assassin grinned. "How did you learn to do that?"

"I have no idea."

"This could be of service to us, Stanford. You have so much untapped potential." The assassin stood up and dusted off his cargo pants. "Let's go. I want to show you something."

Stanford took another look at the shaman before he exited the tent. The man was serene, totally at peace.

As they walked across the sand, the mutants began to gather, flopping on their knees before him like supplicants.

"Give them what they want, Mr. Samuels," said the assassin.

"What do they want?"

"Show them the twin suns."

Stanford looked upon their pained expressions and clenched his fists tightly. He tensed his muscles, feeling the agony of the supplicants, sharing their experience. He ignited his eyes like brilliant stars in the night sky. The mutants shielded their faces from the glare, and when Stanford dimmed the beams, he could see mutants weeping in the shadows.

"This way," said the assassin.

Stanford followed the man into a large tent at the center of the base. Inside, he saw several mutants seated in front of a bank of computer monitors. One of the men was Joshua.

"What do you have for me, Joshua?" asked the assassin.

Joshua spun around in his seat. "Not much, Mr. Dekkar. The little savages haven't been back. There's nothing there now but a mangy helix dog."

Stanford glanced at the assassin. "You mean the children? You knew about them?"

"You will be apprised." The assassin looked back at Joshua. "Do you think the compound has been abandoned?"

Joshua shook his head. "Why would they leave the dog?"

"Maybe they want to throw us off." The assassin sat in one of the seats near the bank of computers. "Are the thermal cameras picking up organic life?"

"The cameras can't penetrate the cement walls, sir."

The assassin looked at Stanford. "What do you propose we do, Mr. Samuels?"

"Why are you asking him?" spat Joshua. "He's not prepped on the intel."

"Stand down, Joshua. Continue to collect images from the aerial drone."

Joshua spun back toward the monitors.

The assassin gestured for Stanford to follow through a rear exit en route to another tent that was connected by a makeshift canvas tunnel.

"You will meet some resistance inside our ranks," said the assassin. "Let it slide off your back. Change is hard for everybody. I'll take care of any persistent issues."

When they arrived inside the new tent, Stanford saw a large rectangular box at the center. The box was draped in a blanket to hide the contents.

"One of our salvage teams picked it up near the dome while you were away. I wanted you to see it before the others."

"Why?"

"You are our leader, Mr. Samuels."

Stanford watched as the assassin removed the cover from the box. Underneath was a cage holding one of the wild children he had seen in the desert. As soon as the child was uncovered, it began to throw its body into the cage, grunting and attempting to chew through the steel bars.

Stanford stared at the boy. "We saw children in the dunes—near the compound."

"There are many, Mr. Samuels."

"What are they doing out there?"

The assassin shook his head. "This particular boy was the runt of a pack of seven. The others escaped into the forest of ferns at the base of Salus. We think they're living in the vegetation. From what we can gather, they travel together much like coyotes. The hunters are all boys so we suspect the girls must remain hidden. I don't know what they're eating, but their food supply will most certainly die out. As you can see, they are uncivilized."

Stanford stepped toward the cage. The boy swiped at him through the bars.

"Have you tried to talk to him?"

"So far he hasn't spoken a word," said the assassin. "I don't know if they have language."

Stanford looked into the boy's eyes. The wild child held his gaze for the briefest of moments and then continued to throw himself into the bars.

"What will you do with him?"

"We haven't gotten that far. We'll discuss it as a team."

"Keep the boy alive," said Stanford.

The assassin turned to face Stanford. "Is that an order?"

"I suppose it is."

The assassin grinned. "It's good to know you're embracing your new role, Mr. Samuels. It's time you got some shut-eye. We'll talk more tomorrow."

The assassin covered the cage with the blanket and they exited the tent.

The child howled in the darkness.

2.10
THE GLASSES

A young boy sat at the edge of a deep crater in the sand while beachgoers scattered in panic. At the bottom of the pit, a woman lay twisted in an unnatural way, her legs bent toward her neck, her facial tissue partially torn to reveal a robot skull beneath.

From behind, the boy heard the cries of his mother.

"Stanford, I told you to stay on the blanket."

Little Stanford pushed his sunglasses up the bridge of his nose and looked up at his mother's worried face. "I came to get the old boy," he pleaded.

His mother yanked him to his feet. "Let's go," she demanded. "We're leaving."

A few feet away, the boy's father was looking on. He was pale under the brilliant glow of the twin suns, and for a brief moment, Stanford wondered why his father's complexion was so absent of color.

The child glanced toward the black and white collie on the opposite side of the pit. "Let's go, old boy."

The dog wagged his tail and shot to his feet, scampering around the hole to follow the family across the sand.

When they reached the sedan in the parking lot, the mother swatted her son firmly across the side of his head, sending his sunglasses toppling to the ground. The boy flinched before stooping to pick them up.

"I told you to wait at the blanket, Stanford."

"I'm sorry, Mom." It took everything he had to fend off tears.

"Get in the car," said his father.

Stanford popped the door handle and scooted into the back seat. The collie jumped in and settled down beside him.

As soon as his parents were secure in the front, the car lifted off the ground and stirred up a thick cloud of dust as it headed for the main thoroughfare back to the southern sector. The traffic was thick and slow going. Police pods came at them from the opposite direction, headed toward the incident on the beach.

Stanford's mother turned to face her son. Her features had not softened. "Do you know why I'm angry with you, Stanford?"

"I think so."

"Leave the boy alone, Stephanie," said his father. "He gets it."

The mother stabbed her husband with a hot glare. "Don't tell me how to feel, Stuart. Any time you want to step in and make an appearance, you are more than welcome."

"Don't patronize me," said his father. "You know how hard I work."

"No, I don't. You're never around to tell me."

Stanford's father slammed his palms against the steering wheel.

There was a long pause before his mother spoke. "I'm sorry," she said. "I didn't mean it." She placed her hand lightly on her husband's shoulder.

The sedan inched forward along the thoroughfare, bumper to bumper; rays of the twin suns beat down through the windshield. The heat inside the car was overwhelming.

"Can you roll down the window, Mom?"

Stanford's mother looked back at her son and smiled. "Of course, honey."

A cool breeze instantly displaced the muggy air.

After a time, the boy said: "Mom, why was that woman in the hole?"

"I don't know, Stanford."

"Is she dead?"

His mother looked at her husband with trembling eyes.

"Yes, she's dead." The response came from his father.

Stanford thought for a moment. "Why did she look like that? Is that what I look like on the inside?"

"Why would you ask such a thing?" said his mother.

"I guess I know I'm different."

"You are perfectly normal, Stanford. Don't be silly."

His father spoke up. "Forget about the woman, son. Put her out of your mind. She's not like you. You are a normal boy."

"Am I, Dad?"

"Yes. Never think of her again. Do you hear me?"

"Okay, Dad."

He could hear his father exhale deeply.

Stanford stared out at the traffic, but his mind was locked on the image of the woman. "What happens after you die?" he asked. "Where do you go?"

"You get eaten by worms," said his father.

Stanford's mother interjected. "Please, Stuart, don't say that."

"What happens, Mom?"

Stanford's mother looked back at her son again. "Nobody knows for sure, honey. I like to think that you go to the most beautiful place you can imagine."

"What place is that?"

"It depends. It's different for everybody."

Stanford thought for a moment. "I think the best place ever is the farm where we got the old boy." He scratched the collie behind the ears.

"That's a wonderful place," said his mother with a smile. "Do you remember the mountains we passed through to get there?"

"The roads were scary. We were really high up."

Stanford's mom chuckled. "Yes, we certainly were. I'm surprised I was brave enough to drive you there without your father." She was silent for a moment. "Do you remember when we stopped at the waterfall?"

Stanford nodded. "Yes. I liked it there."

"I did too," said his mother.

The memory rekindled the excitement inside him. "The water was so cold!"

Stanford's mother laughed.

There was a pause and Stanford spoke again. "But I lost my sunglasses."

"It's okay, honey. We replaced them."

His mother's face was so beautiful and comforting. Even though he knew she had been angry with him for losing his glasses, she didn't show it. He wished she would look at him like that forever.

"I wish I didn't need the glasses."

"It's just a part of who you are," said his mother. "You are a special boy. Your father and I love you very much."

As the hover car came to a dead stop in traffic, Stanford's father twisted his head around to face his son. "Don't spend a second feeling ashamed for being unique. It's what makes you special, do you hear me?"

Stanford nodded. "Yes, Dad."

"Never forget it."

"I won't."

His mother reached into the back seat and squeezed her son's hand. "I love you, Stanford Samuels. You have so much to offer the world. You'll be a king one day."

Stanford watched a tear trickle down his mother's cheek.

"Don't be sad, Mom."

She squeezed his hand again. "I'm not, baby. These are tears of joy."

He saw his father reach across to hold his mother's hand.

Stanford felt safe.

2.11
NEW BEGINNING

Stanford woke on the floor of the big tent. When he sat upright he brushed the sand off his cheeks and noticed the cot on the far side was empty—the shaman was no longer there. As he struggled to regain his bearings, the assassin burst through the flap.

"Stanford, get up. The shaman is dead."

Before Stanford could focus his eyes, the assassin was gone. He got to his feet and made his way to the exit. He could hear the sound of chanting on the opposite side of the canvas.

Outside, he saw the assembly of mutants surrounding a funeral pyre.

"Piss on the Patron, piss on the Patron, piss on the Patron . . ."

The voices of the mutants echoed through the darkness.

The assassin quickly approached. "You need to say something, Mr. Samuels. This is the passing of the torch. You need to stand before your congregation and give them hope."

Stanford could feel his eyes growing hot. "What am I supposed to say? I don't know the first thing about being a leader."

"Of course you don't, Stanford. All you need to do is appease the crowd. Don't screw it up."

"What should I do?"

The assassin pushed Stanford toward the pyre. "Make your eyes glow."

Stanford was suddenly next to the funeral pyre, with the attention of hundreds of mutants directly on him.

He scanned the crowd. He could see the resident mother amongst the spectators, cradling the dead android's baby. He felt a wave of anxiety wash over him, nearly drowning him. He cleared his throat and tried to settle his quivering voice.

"Mutants, we are gathered here to pay respect to a great leader—a man who has stood before us since the very beginning—a man who brought us strength and wisdom."

Several mutants began muttering amongst themselves, ignoring Stanford's speech. The crowd seemed disengaged, rattled by the death of the shaman.

Stanford looked at the assassin.

The assassin motioned for him to continue.

"There is only one man who has stared into the eyes of the Patron and stood his ground. That man is the shaman. This is not a funeral but an awakening. As a group, we have inherited his power and will bravely continue his mission. We too, will stare at the Patron with unblinking eyes. We will refuse to be denied what is rightfully ours."

The assembly of mutants continued to chatter, barely hearing his words.

Stanford glanced upon the crowd and squeezed his fists into tight balls. He tensed his shoulders and his abdomen. He pressed his eyelids together like steel traps, and when he finally opened them, he lit the night with his brilliant rays.

A hush instantly fell over the crowd.

"Tonight we pay our final respects to the shaman. I won't pretend that I've known this man for very long, but I owe my life to him. When I was ready to give everything up, alone in the colony, the shaman took me in. He brought me back from the dead and welcomed me into his community. If it weren't for him, I wouldn't be here right now."

The beams from Stanford's eyes were blinding.

"It is my pleasure to be a member of your family . . . to have a second chance. From this point on, you can count on me to do my very best to provide the leadership you have been accustomed to. I can't promise to fill the void left by this man. I don't have the shaman's wisdom or experience. But I can guarantee my devotion. I can guarantee to lead you to Salus."

Stanford turned toward the pyre. The shaman rested peacefully in clean burial robes.

"There is no end. There is only a new beginning."

With that, the pyre ignited in a giant blaze, bringing heat and light to the desert.

The spectators watched in awe.

Stanford looked toward the assassin. The assassin nodded.

The crowd began to chant before the raging fire.

"Piss on the Patron, piss on the Patron, piss on the Patron . . ."

Stanford watched on. His eyes burned bright. This was his mission now. He needed to lead them to Salus and find his son. He had no other purpose. Everything he had known was gone. And he didn't care about it anyway. His emotions were numb.

All he cared about was lighting the way through the darkness. All he cared about was finding his boy.

The assassin stood beside him. "Now it begins."

PART V

THE PROJECT

2.12
THE CHAMBER

Doctor Le was seated before a computer monitor showing a magnified image of a fern spore. The spore was shaped like an irregular oval with fine hairs protruding from its exterior membrane.

Standing behind the doctor was his partner, Doctor Eggers, along with another man in a dark, tailored suit. All three watched the screen with interest.

"The morphological data shows nothing unusual," said Doctor Le. "The characteristics are what we'd expect from any other classification of ferns, with the exception of the fortress-like outer membrane."

The man in the dark suit squinted at the monitor. "After all you've subjected it to, how could it not show the slightest hint of trauma?" The acronym PAD was stitched on his breast pocket.

Doctor Le flashed a look at his partner and then back at the visitor. "Other than the release of abscisic acid, I cannot say. The plant has an unnatural defense mechanism. It's like a suit of armor."

"And yet you were able to separate the leaf from the parent plant. How curious."

Doctor Le turned back to the computer monitor. "It

seems to have a mind of its own. What's most fascinating is the production of O2. Watch what happens when I introduce heat to the spore."

Doctor Le placed a Petri dish containing the mysterious sample onto a hotplate and adjusted the knob.

The men observed the screen intently.

A few moments passed but the magnified oval remained unchanged.

"What am I waiting for?" asked the man from the PAD.

Doctor Eggers interjected. "It can withstand immense amounts of pressure. The pain threshold is something that far exceeds anything we've witnessed before. It's almost preternatural."

Doctor Le turned the dial on the hotplate to achieve maximum power. The sides of the Petri dish began to sag as it slowly melted onto the heat source, creating a column of thick, black smoke that filled the laboratory with the pungent scent of burnt plastic.

The fire alarm began to sound.

"Turn it off," demanded the man in the suit.

"Just watch the screen!" bellowed Doctor Le.

As the plastic sizzled, the image on the monitor began to change. Other shapes came into frame, taking residence amongst the oval.

"Note the appearance of the O2. It manifests under all types of adverse conditions. I was even able to coax it out when I hit the spore with a hammer. But it seems to react to heat in the most significant way."

"Remarkable," said the man from the PAD, raising his voice to combat the incessant racket of the alarm.

The men turned their eyes upon the methodical flame as it consumed the last remnants of the Petri dish.

"As you have witnessed," said Doctor Le, also speaking loudly, "the oxygen forms at a tremendous rate—much faster than photosynthesis in nature. The molecules are unstable, making them highly reactive."

"Yes, I see. How do we proceed?" asked the man.

Without warning, the overhead sprinklers activated, sending all three men back-pedaling to avoid the shower.

"I believe it's time we informed the Patron," said Doctor Le. "These ferns are able to create breathable oxygen on command without the addition of natural sunlight."

"I can barely hear you," said the man from the PAD. "Did you say the molecules are breathable? If they are unstable, as you readily admit, then making such a claim seems rather dubious without further testing."

Doctor Le glanced at his partner. "Doctor Eggers, if you will do the honors."

"Of course." Doctor Eggers removed several large fronds from a storage cupboard and sealed them inside a carrying case.

"To test our hypothesis, Doctor Eggers and I have arranged for an Alice unit to serve as our subject. Would you follow us to the hyperbaric chamber, please?"

"I'd be happy to get away from this blistering noise," said the man in the suit.

The men exited the laboratory, escaping the alarm into a quiet hallway. Doctor Le led them down the corridor to a door marked: *Nurturing Room: Authorized Personnel Only.*

He knocked.

Within moments, a woman in a nurse's uniform answered.

"Good day," said Doctor Le. "Would you please tell Alice that we await her presence?"

The nurse stood back to allow the men inside. "She's finishing with an offspring. She shouldn't be long. You can wait in here."

The men entered the dark room and sat down in front of a one-way glass mirror. Doctor Eggers set the case with the fern on his lap.

On the other side of the glass the men had a view of a massive room housing row upon row of incubators. Several nurses were making their way through the aisles, opening the lids of the capsules and removing the children from within. They held each child for precisely one minute against their bosom, rocking gently before setting the tiny newborns carefully back into the incubators and moving on to the next capsule to repeat the process. The children were completely content; not a hint of fuss.

The nurse in the waiting room smiled as she turned to face the guests. "It's beautiful, isn't it? Nurturing is an essential part of every child's neurological growth. It's a critical piece to the formation of language and social behavior. Ninety percent of brain development takes place in the first three years of life, did you know that? Before the Patron approved the nurturing program, the children in this ward were not able to get the care they deserved."

"That's heartwarming," said Doctor Le, "but where is Alice?"

"She's in the quarantine ward," said the nurse, "tending to the other incubator. She shouldn't be long."

"We're on a tight schedule. This man is from the PAD. He is very busy, as are we. Would you mind summoning her?"

The nurse's smile evaporated. "I appreciate the importance of your work, Doctor, but I must insist that you respect the importance of mine. Interrupting the nurturing process can have significant long-term effects on a child's development. We won't make the same mistakes again. Alice should be here any moment now."

Doctor Le exhaled deeply. He peered through the one-way glass to watch the crew of nurturers opening and closing capsules, gently rocking and caressing the fragile infants. When he looked back, he saw the waiting room door open, introducing a sliver of light from the hallway.

Alice stood in the doorway, adorning a tight-fitting red dress. "I'm ready, gentlemen," she said.

The men accompanied Alice down the hall to another room with a hyperbaric chamber at its center.

"This man is from the PAD," said Doctor Le.

"Pleased to meet you," said Alice.

"Likewise," said the man.

"And of course you know Doctor Eggers."

"What will you have me do?" asked Alice. Her red lipstick parted to reveal flawless white teeth.

Doctor Eggers set the carrying case on a countertop and turned back to face the android. "We would like you to enter the chamber, Alice. All you have to do is stand inside; nothing more than that."

Doctor Le addressed the man in the dark suit. "The chamber has been reverse programmed to evacuate itself entirely of oxygen, creating a vacuum environment."

The Alice unit looked between the three men with a degree of concern.

"Do you understand the experiment?" asked Doctor Le.

"Yes, I think I do," said the man from the PAD.

"Good." He looked back at Alice. "Please step inside."

"But what will happen to me?"

"This is an experiment," said Doctor Le. "I have a hypothesis that works out favorably for you. Now kindly enter the chamber."

Alice's eyes were wide. She walked slowly toward the chamber door, pausing several times for reassurance.

"It's all in the name of science, my dear," said Doctor Le. "Where would we be without experiments just like this? Go ahead. Get inside."

Alice moved into the half-sphere. Her body was visible through an acrylic viewing window.

"Please observe the Alice unit while O2 gas is removed from the chamber," announced Doctor Le. "Watch for signs of asphyxiation."

Alice was completely still as she stared out the window. The look on her face was void of expression.

"What if the experiment fails?" asked the man from the PAD. "Have you inquired about older test models from the disassembling station? The Alice unit is still a valuable commodity. I doubt very much that the Patron will look kindly upon gratuitous killing of his assets."

"Units predating Alice are not designed with a sophisticated enough nervous system to provide accurate data," said Doctor Le. "Alice mimics human responses almost as if she is human herself. I will take full responsibility for the results."

The man glanced at the chamber. "It's your neck, not mine. Please proceed."

Doctor Le nodded at Doctor Eggers as he initiated the chamber with a remote keypad. The room filled with the sound of a deflating balloon. All three men watched Alice through the acrylic window. She was stoic at first, but within moments her cheeks appeared sunken, her lips began to enlarge.

"Her eyes are bulging," said the man from the PAD. His voice registered a note of trepidation.

"It's too soon," said Doctor Le. "Give it more time."

Inside the chamber, Alice clutched her throat with one hand and banged against the window with the other. Her protruding eyes trembled with fear. She opened her mouth to speak, but there were no words.

"We're losing her, doctors! Terminate the experiment!"

Doctor Eggers finally removed a fern frond from the carrying case, followed by a blowtorch from the pocket of his lab coat. The torch, small enough to fit comfortably in his hand, produced an intense blue flame that he held just beneath the leaf.

When the frond began to smoke, Doctor Eggers placed it in a drawer that pulled out from the exterior shell of the chamber. "Just observe the android," he said, sending the smoking fern inside the half-sphere.

The Alice unit collapsed to the floor; her legs jerked as she lost muscle control. Her skin was stark white, her lips swollen to twice their normal size.

The men watched Alice's body kick out the last remnants of vitality before becoming stiff and lifeless. The breathing mechanism in her chest ceased to function.

The man in the suit looked away in disgust. "This is what you had me see?"

Doctor Le walked toward the viewing window to get a closer look. "She's not gone. Look now."

The Alice unit began to stir. Her fingers twitched; her legs began to shift. She appeared momentarily disoriented before sitting upright.

The men watched her walk toward the inner drawer and examine the emerald green fern frond that continued to release a thin wisp of smoke. She sniffed it like a flower and looked through the acrylic window. "Can I come out now?"

The men looked at one another and laughed.

The color had returned to Alice's complexion. Her bright red lipstick remained flawless.

Doctor Le pressed a button to open the hatch.

"Did it work?" asked Alice.

Doctor Le took her hand to help her out of the chamber. "Yes," he said. "I'd say the experiment was quite successful." He looked at the man from the PAD. "Are you satisfied?"

The man smiled broadly. "Indeed. It's time we inform the Patron of your findings."

"Well done," said Doctor Le to his partner.

Doctor Eggers was positively beaming, while the Alice unit appeared as sprightly as ever.

2.13
WILD CHILD

Stanford entered the tent and stood quietly in the dark. He tensed his muscles to activate his eye-beams, casting a spotlight on the cage with the blanket covering. He listened for a moment, but the cage was completely silent. He moved forward and removed the blanket.

Lying on the floor, sound asleep, was the naked body of the wild child. Stanford dimmed his eyes and sat down in the sand nearby. He watched the boy's chest rising and falling, his mouth slightly agape to suck in the crisp night air. Stanford slid the blanket through the bars of the cage. He wanted to cover the child, to subdue the quivering, but the boy was just out of his reach.

He felt a sense of helplessness as he watched on. The boy's face was peaceful beneath the dirt and grime. He looked as innocent as any other small child in need of food and shelter. Perhaps he had gotten lost during the exodus. His family would be desperately searching.

Stanford felt a fluttering in his chest. Was this how he used to feel for his own child? He had no way of remembering, but his instincts told him that he needed to do everything in his power to keep the boy safe.

I will help you find your way.

The boy jerked suddenly, as if woken by Stanford's inner thoughts. His eyes shot open, and he scurried across to the far side of the cage, tucking his legs up to his chest and hiding his face behind his knees. Sounds that resembled growling reverberated in the boy's lungs.

Stanford took a moment, for he too had been startled, before reaching through the bars to retrieve the blanket. He walked carefully around the perimeter of the cage, moving with slow, deliberate strides so as not to appear threatening. The boy was rocking back and forth in the tucked position, his face still hidden. The sound of pure terror continued to permeate the tent.

Stanford pushed the blanket through the bars and dropped it next to the child.

The boy's head shot up to reveal wide, trembling eyes. Once again, he scurried across to the opposite side of the cage, back to his original position, growling and baring teeth. The boy pulled his legs close to his chest and tried to hide from the perceived threat.

Stanford stood still for a moment. He could see the child's body shivering. He knew it was not a reaction to the cold—it was a response to fear.

Repeating the same pattern, Stanford retrieved the blanket from inside the cage and walked around the perimeter to where the boy was rocking back and forth. This time he pushed the blanket through the bars and backed off.

He sat in the sand and watched for several minutes before the child finally lifted his head and looked at the blanket on the floor a few feet away. The boy shot a glance at Stanford, gauging his proximity.

Stanford didn't move a muscle.

With extreme caution, the child stretched his arm to take hold of the blanket. Once he got it in his grasp, he wrapped it around his body and returned to the same position, rocking back and forth, creating a kind of warm cocoon to hide in.

Stanford stood up and walked toward the exit. He could feel his eyes growing hot as the copper activated in his irises, and for the first time since his body had been anesthetized, he felt a strong emotion welling up inside him. There was no mistaking the identity of the emotion. It was anger.

He exited the tent quickly and made his way toward the headquarters. Supplicants raced out of their tents and threw themselves at his feet, but he stepped over them like they were not there. Adrenaline was pumping through his veins. His past may have been numbed, but his present was humming with powerful sensations. He was furious that the boy had been treated like an animal, left in the cage in the cold without so much as a blanket. He needed to protect this boy, because it seemed nobody else would. He would not allow the child to be abandoned.

When he reached the main tent, he pushed aggressively through the flap and made a beeline toward the bank of computers.

A group of soldiers sat in front of the monitors, the assassin and Joshua among them.

The assassin spun around in his chair. "Mr. Samuels, we were just about to give you a wakeup call. You look rather agitated. Were your sleeping quarters not satisfactory?"

Stanford trained his eye-beams directly at the assassin. "Why is that boy still naked in the cage?"

The assassin blocked the rays with his hands. "It's hard to have a conversation when you're blinding me, Stanford. Would you mind turning those down a notch?"

"I asked you a question, Markus."

"The boy is in good hands. We are monitoring him closely. He's perfectly comfortable."

"The boy is naked and he's cold. You know more than anyone what it's like to be young and scared, held in a strange place against your will. I expected compassion from you. I demand you stop treating him like an animal."

"He *is* an animal." The voice came from Joshua.

Stanford shifted his glowing eyes to Joshua. The rays were so intense, the mutant nearly toppled backward in his chair.

"What is wrong with you, Stanford?"

"Find the boy some clothes immediately. If you want me as your leader, you better start following my orders. Do you hear me, Joshua?"

Joshua looked to the assassin for instructions.

"You heard him," said the assassin. "Get the boy some clothes."

Joshua stood up from his seat and marched out of the tent without another word.

"Would you mind dimming your eyes, Mr. Samuels?" said the assassin. "I appreciate your passion, but I won't be of much use if I'm permanently blind."

Stanford took a deep breath and his eyes dimmed automatically.

"Thank you," said the assassin. "I'm sorry. You are right about the boy. It was insensitive."

Stanford sat down in the chair vacated by Joshua. His body felt weak as his anger dissipated into the cool air.

"I'm willing to help you," he said, "but we need to keep our humanity for as long as we possibly can."

The assassin smiled. "Indeed. I'm pleased you joined our team, Mr. Samuels. You bring a perspective that we have been lacking."

"You didn't give me a choice."

"Things have a way of working out." The assassin turned back to the computer monitor. "Since you're here, I might as well get you up to speed. Do you feel up to it?"

Stanford nodded and turned his calm eyes to the monitor.

"We've had an aerial drone monitoring the compound thirty miles outside of Salus for several days," said the assassin. "There are some images I want you to take a look at."

The assassin entered a command in the touchscreen, bringing up an overhead shot of a massive military transport vehicle with caterpillar tracks parked outside the front of the compound. The vehicle was segmented between the front and back end, resembling a kind of giant desert arthropod. A tarpaulin was stretched from the rear of truck to the entrance of the building, hiding whatever traveled in between.

"That's a Sand Crawler," said the assassin. "It's a surface vehicle used by the Militia for operations in the outer boundaries."

"What kind of operations?"

"They were deployed primarily in the first war to sniff out terrorist cells hiding amongst the ash dunes. They are particularly effective vehicles because they have an indestructible exoskeleton; they move in a rectilinear fashion over the sand, almost completely without sound because the engine doesn't employ thruster technology. They are like a silent predator. We haven't seen a Sand Crawler in action for quite some time."

"What's it doing there?"

"We don't know. That shot was taken three days ago, just a few hours after the exodus announcement in the mutant colony. We can confirm that it appeared at least two more times since. Whatever it is they are moving between the Sand Crawler and the compound, they don't want us to know about. The tarp is insulated so we can't even scan for body heat."

"Where is the vehicle now?"

"Out of the range of the drone. Sand Crawlers are out-fitted with an anti-tracking device. We know it went west toward Salus, but we lost the signal."

The assassin hit a key on the computer and gener-ated another image. The photo was dark and pixilated, but Stanford could vaguely make out the figure of a woman standing out front of the main door of the compound. The woman's dark hair was tied in a tight bun, reminding him immediately of Ilsa K.

"The infrared can't get a clear image," said the assassin, "which indicates that the female lacks body heat."

Stanford thought for a moment. "She's an android."

"Yes, Mr. Samuels, but all the generational models we have encountered so far have emitted some degree of heat energy. A processor creates heat, and without a processor there is nothing to drive the system. She's different."

Stanford exhaled deeply.

"Are you okay, Stanford?"

"Yes. Go on, please."

"I've arranged a convoy," said the assassin. "We need to find out what's going on in there. Whatever new model of android is hiding inside those walls, our job is to eliminate them. This will be a full-out assault."

"What if the Sand Crawler returns?"

"Then we'll have a hell of a fight on our hands."

Stanford glanced back at the photo. The female's resemblance to Ilsa K was undeniable.

"Are you feeling up to this, Stanford?"

Stanford looked back at the assassin's mangled features. The copper began to circle his pupils like the beginnings of a dust storm.

The assassin patted him on the shoulder. "Let's go to work."

2.14
THE COMPOUND

From his hiding place behind a sand dune, Stanford stared through the infrared binoculars at the rectangular compound in the desert.

"What do you see?" asked the assassin.

The exterior of the building was vacant. He scanned across the empty terrain at wide open space.

"There's nothing there."

"Let's get our gear," said the assassin.

They retreated to the military vehicles parked in a shallow crater a short distance away. When they arrived, the assassin tapped the top of his head to signal the soldiers inside the trucks.

All the doors opened at once, spilling the Tech Terrorists onto the sand. The soldiers covered their faces with bandanas to protect their lungs from the nuclear dust.

The assassin approached the rear of a vehicle and popped the trunk. He reached inside and removed an assault rifle and a portable sonar unit. "Mr. Samuels. We have plenty of weaponry. Please make a selection."

Stanford stayed where he was. "I don't need your weapons," he said.

"Mr. Samuels, we are going into a hostile environment. I suggest you arm yourself. We may not be able to protect you."

Stanford stood motionless.

The assassin slung the rifle over his shoulder and approached Stanford quickly. "I'm growing weary of your reluctance. Whether you like it or not, you are now in a position to lead the Tech Terrorists into battle. We've gone over this. Don't be a fool."

Stanford stepped toward the trunk and reached for a stubby but solid handgun with a double-barrel. It fit his hand perfectly. "I'm ready, Mr. Dekkar."

The assassin looked at the gun and smiled. "Lead the way, Mr. Samuels."

As Stanford led the brigade along the sand toward the compound, he felt in the breast pocket of his panda jacket for his double-tinted sunglasses. He could hear his mother's voice echoing in his ears.

"Your eyes are extremely sensitive to light. You need to protect them. The glasses are the most important thing you will own. You need to wear them whenever you leave the house, especially on extra sunny days. Don't lose them. Do you hear me, Stanford?"

Stanford remembered sitting next to his mother in the car as they traveled through the mountain pass on the way to the collie farm. Out the side window, he saw the gush of a blue-green waterfall dropping over the edge of a high cliff, collecting in a churning stream off the side of the road.

"Look at that, Mom!"

His mother pulled the hover car into a shoulder. "Do you want to cool off, Stanford?"

"Yes, Mom!"

They got out of the car and raced toward the frothy

cascade. As soon as Stanford was close, he could feel the cool mist landing on his face.

"Be careful, Stanford. Don't get too close."

"I won't, Mom."

Little Stanford leaned over the edge of the bank and reached his hand into the pool. The water was ice cold. It felt refreshing on his warm skin.

"We should bring Dad here."

He shuffled forward so he could submerge his arm up to the elbow, but his sunglasses came dislodged and fell into the stream. For a brief moment he glimpsed the reflection of his naked mutant eyes in the water before stretching his arm as far as it would go, frantically attempting to retrieve the glasses.

"Don't move, Stanford!"

"I lost them, Mom."

The image of his mother was distorted by his tears.

"I know, baby. It's okay . . . we can replace them . . ."

Now, as Stanford marched across the sandy terrain, he took one last look at his glasses before tossing them into a dune. Almost instantly they were covered over by a layer of swirling dust.

They're gone for good, he thought. *They are no longer a part of me.*

Every step forward felt like he was leaving something behind—but it no longer hurt. The fern had cut the umbilical cord to his past. There were no more forks in the road. No turning back. Now there was only one direction to run.

He gripped the gun and heard the voice of the assassin.

"Turn on your high beams, Mr. Samuels. The sonar is detecting movement up ahead."

Stanford squeezed the handle of the gun, feeling tension in his arms all the way to his shoulders and neck. As his legs churned across the desert, he realized that the person he used to be was a mere shadow that grew fainter by the minute. It was as if he had been buried in the nuclear ash along with his glasses, only to emerge as a leader of men. He felt powerful.

"Quickly, Stanford! It's closing fast."

His eyes ignited the darkness.

Directly ahead, a helix dog was snarling and barreling in his direction. The haunches rippled with muscle and silvery sinew.

"Watch out!" screamed the assassin.

Stanford aimed the double-barrel at the dog, and with the precision of a trained sniper, fired a single shot. The dog exploded, sending metal parts flying in all directions. The soldiers took cover to avoid the shrapnel.

When Stanford looked back at the group, he saw the assassin's wide eyes staring back.

"You hit the sweet spot, Mr. Samuels. How did you learn to shoot like that?"

Stanford glanced at his gun silently. With every passing moment, he was becoming more like the physicals. The survival instinct was growing strong, making him capable of things he could not have conceived of before now. Perhaps the warrior had always resided within him. He would never know. All he knew was that he would need more of the same if he hoped to find his son. The mission would require great strength.

Looking forward, the rectangular compound was within range of his eye-beams.

The assassin turned to address the crew. "We've reached the target. You all know the mission. Once we're inside, the only objective is to annihilate the synthetics. All other occupants, whoever they are, are irrelevant. I don't want a single android left alive. Do you understand?"

The soldiers performed a silent salute.

"Be vigilant, mutants. It's time to piss on the Patron."

The brigade rushed through the final stretch of desert until they reached the front of the compound. They were stealthy, moving as one.

One of the mutants began rigging an explosive device to the front door. A quick, soundless blast ensued, and the group was inside in an instant. They moved in single file down a dimly lit cement hallway that terminated at a steel door. The same mutant began to rig another explosive, but Stanford stepped forward and took hold of the door handle, finding it unlocked. He twisted the knob and cracked the door slightly ajar.

The assassin shrugged and made a signal to enter.

The mutants were through the door before Stanford had a chance to move. He dimmed his eyes and followed.

Inside was a room as large as a warehouse. Cots were arranged in aisles, each with fresh white linen and surgical EM lamps hanging overhead. Every cot was occupied by an unconscious patient dressed in a white gown. The room was empty otherwise.

The assassin made a signal to initiate a search.

As the crew went off in different directions, the assassin leaned in close to Stanford. "They know we're here."

"How do you know?

"They sent the dog. They are probably watching us right now."

Stanford scanned the warehouse. All he saw were the mutant soldiers executing the search command. He felt a shiver creep up his spine.

"Maybe we should fall back. This could be an ambush."

The assassin shook his head. "It's too late for that, Stanford."

"What do we do?"

"We wait. Let's see who blinks first."

Stanford felt his heart rate double. He watched one of the soldiers patrolling the aisles of cots and remembered searching for his own child in the incubators. He was frantic back then—a father searching desperately for his son, clinging to a thread of hope, but fearing the worst outcome imaginable. The feelings of pain and loss had been cleansed from his system, but he could not ignore the pull of the cots. He needed to join the search party to establish a sense of self-worth. This was his team. Standing on the sidelines made him feel useless.

The assassin grabbed his arm. "The area isn't secure, Stanford. You need to stay out of the line of fire."

"I can't just stand here."

"Let my men do their work. The terrorists are trained for these operations. Your place is here, next to me."

"You want me to be a part of this, so let me go," said Stanford. He pulled his arm free and walked toward the cots.

Making his way through the aisles, he stared into the faces of the unconscious patients. He saw cleft lips and freckled skin; chin dimples and widow's peaks; some with red hair, others with blond. Each of them was bathed in the glow of the overhead surgical lights, all peaceful and serene. These were faces of unconscious mutants, herded together like cattle in a barn. Was this the slaughter house?

How could such insignificant imperfections have resulted in this end? If not for the occasional flickering of an eyelid or twitch of a hand, Stanford would have presumed them all dead.

Continuing through the aisles, he paused when he came upon a familiar face. It was the visage of an old man, beaten and weathered by time. Deep cracks in the forehead suggested a lifetime of struggle that even Stanford could not match, and yet he felt a kinship with the man that could only be borne from a similar disease. He placed his hand on the man's emaciated chest, feeling the barely functioning lungs within.

The assassin was already on his way over. "What's going on, Mr. Samuels?"

Stanford lowered the EM lamp to better illuminate the patient's face. Now he was sure. This was his old friend from the factory, the man with haemochromatosis.

"Do you know this man, Stanford?"

Stanford leaned close to the cot. "Wake up, Iron Man. Can you hear me?"

The old man was motionless.

"It's me, Iron Man. It's Saturn. You're safe now. We're going to take you out of here." Stanford looked at the assassin. "We need to take him back to the base."

"Stanford, we must execute the mission."

Stanford's copper rings began to swirl.

The assassin took the hint. "Okay. We'll get him out. But we need to complete a full sweep of the base first."

Stanford glanced back at his old friend. "Just rest now, Iron Man. Everything will be okay."

The startling blast of automatic gunfire echoed through the room.

The assassin turned toward the sound, rifle at the ready. "Stay here with your friend, Mr. Samuels."

All of the soldiers quickly disappeared into the shadows at the rear of the warehouse.

"I'm coming," said Stanford. He looked back at the old man. "I'll be back."

Stanford was right behind the assassin. His eyes ignited automatically to light a path across the cement floor. They moved quickly down a corridor at the far end of the warehouse, following the sound of the firefight all the way to a door that was slightly ajar. The sounds of gunfire ceased. The hallway was conspicuously silent.

The assassin motioned for Stanford to stop. He stepped toward the door and took a moment before kicking it open.

Inside, a squadron of mutant soldiers, including Joshua, stood with assault rifles slung over their shoulders. At their feet were the remains of a dozen or more mutilated androids. Metallic body parts were strewn everywhere; black fluid painted the walls. Many of the appendages were still twitching and smoldering with dark smoke.

Joshua wore a look of great satisfaction. "We got 'em, sir."

The assassin stepped inside.

"They were holed up in here," said Joshua, "probably hiding until we left. They were a bunch of white coats. We turned them into scrap metal."

"Are there others?" asked the assassin.

"No sir, the rest of the compound is clean."

"Nothing on the infrared?"

Joshua shook his head. "No sir."

Stanford stepped over a decapitated robot skull as he entered the room. The synthetic tissue had been seared off; black fluid drained from the ear and nostril holes. "Did you think to ask them what they were doing here before you opened fire?" he asked.

Joshua glared back. "Our mission isn't to ask why, Mr. Samuels, only to annihilate."

"All right," said the assassin. "Let's clear out."

As they walked back down the hall toward the warehouse, Stanford pulled the assassin to the side. "We can't leave those patients here, Mr. Dekkar."

The assassin placed his hand on Stanford's shoulder. "Mr. Samuels, you make things a hell of a lot more complicated, but a wise man once told me that we have to maintain our humanity for as long as we can."

Stanford nodded. "Thank you."

"I'll radio for a transport truck," said the assassin. "No patient will be left behind. And don't worry, we'll take good care of your friend."

As they continued down the hallway, the assassin spoke again. "How do you feel about your first real combat mission, Stanford?"

Stanford hesitated. Seeing the carnage in the other room made him realize he still had a long way to go to become a terrorist.

The assassin smiled. "It is never pleasant, Stanford, but it will get easier."

Stanford turned his head to the side.

"What's wrong?" asked the assassin.

Stanford looked at a side door and drew his gun.

The assassin cocked his rifle and gestured for Stanford to stand back. He put his ear to the door and listened. After a moment he stepped back and broke through the door with his foot.

Stanford stared into the room. In the spotlight cast from his eyes, he illuminated a woman in a white medical coat. He noticed her brown hair tied up in a tight bun. He recognized her from the digital photo.

"Get on your knees," demanded the assassin, bursting into the room with gusto.

The woman dropped to the floor and put her hands on her head.

Stanford stepped forward, seeing her pupils constrict to the size of pinpricks.

"She evaded the infrared, Stanford. She's one of the new synthetics."

Stanford lowered his gun and examined her at close range. "Who are you?" he asked.

The woman stared back with lifeless eyes. There was not a hint of humanity inside her.

The assassin pressed the tip of his rifle against her temple. "Answer the question," he demanded.

Finally, the woman spoke. "I'm a Class-5." Her voice was flat.

"What is your purpose?" asked Stanford.

"We are scientists. I was assigned to the Project like the rest of the Class-5s you butchered."

Stanford glanced at the assassin before addressing the android again. "What project?"

The woman appeared completely devoid of emotion.

The assassin nudged the tip of his gun into her temple to elicit a response.

"Are there more of you inside the compound?" asked Stanford.

The woman stared up the rifle at the assassin. She

showed no fear. The look on her face seemed to welcome death. "It's time you kill me," she said.

The assassin cocked the hammer on the weapon.

Stanford stepped toward him. "Let her live," he said.

"What are you talking about, Mr. Samuels?"

"She works for the Patron. She's been inside Salus."

The assassin let his finger off the trigger as if it stretched every ounce of his will power to the limit. He lowered the barrel and stared at the android's pale face before addressing Stanford. "I'll call for a transport truck."

When the assassin was gone, Stanford trained his eyes on the android. There was no soul behind the constricted pupils. He wondered what she was thinking and what she feared more than death.

"Get up," he said.

2.15
THE CLASS-5

Stanford watched the old man being loaded into the back of the transport vehicle, followed by a procession of other cots bearing unconscious mutant patients. The emotions he once associated with his old friend had been stolen, but he maintained the ability to feel compassion for a fellow human being in need. He refused to accept that his friend's life would end at the hands of mad scientists. He shuddered at the thought that any of these people should perish in this place. Dying alone in the mutant colony seemed like a far better option by comparison.

What are they doing out here with the mutants?

When the final cot was loaded, the rear hatch closed and Stanford headed back to the escort vehicle. The assassin was waiting for him.

"We have the android shackled in the back seat, Mr. Samuels. I have arranged for you to ride in the other transport with your friend."

"Thank you, Mr. Dekkar, but I prefer to ride in this vehicle. It will give me a chance to question the android."

"We'll have lots of time for questioning, Mr. Samuels."

"I'll ride in this vehicle," Stanford repeated.

"Very well."

Both men jumped aboard.

The assassin took his seat and addressed the driver. "Get us out of here, Jack."

"Yes, sir."

As the thrusters ignited in the undercarriage, a helix dog appeared in the range of the headlights. The dog charged across a sand dune and then stopped. It stared in the direction of the convoy before retreating with its tail between its legs.

The mutants laughed.

"Go home, mad dog!" screeched the assassin.

Stanford thought of the old boy. The usual pang of sadness was no longer present, but he hoped the dog was okay, wherever he was.

I hope he's warm.

He glanced in the back seat and saw the android wrapped in chains. Her brown hair had been released from the bun and fell upon her thin shoulders like frayed strands of yarn. Up close, she no longer reminded him of Ilsa K. The android's hair was lighter and wispier; her eyes looked more like Glenda's. But it was an illusion. This was not Glenda. This was not Ilsa K. This was something else entirely.

She averted her stare.

"Look at me," said Stanford.

The android disregarded him.

Stanford felt his irises growing hot as the tension in his body increased. "Look at me," he repeated, firmly. "If you don't answer my questions, I can't protect you."

The android slowly turned to absorb his image.

"My name is Stanford Samuels. What do I call you?"

"Who cares what we call her?" said the assassin.

108

Stanford shot his beams at the assassin and then back at the android.

"I have been assigned the name Winifred," she said, squinting.

Stanford dimmed his irises. "Tell me about the Class-5s, Winifred. When were you were manufactured?"

"I am incapable of recall. The Class-5 hippocampus is nonfunctional. I will be of little use to you as a prisoner."

The assassin interjected again. "Why are you wasting your time with formalities, Mr. Samuels? You're not on a date. Ask her how she's able to evade detection from the infrared."

The android stared straight ahead. "We are not like the old units. We were designed for super-efficiency, with no energy emissions of any kind."

"It's a camouflage," said the assassin. "I know a military unit when I see one."

Stanford turned impatiently toward the assassin. "Mr. Dekkar, would you please allow me to ask the questions?"

The assassin got up from his seat. "I'm done listening to this anyway. I'll be in the front if you need me."

Stanford watched him go. He knew how difficult it was for a man like the assassin to disobey his natural instincts. From the time he left home as a child, he had been training to fight the enemy. Now, with the target sitting right next to him, he was expected to control the impulses that defined him. Stanford didn't begrudge the man for showing his frustration.

He turned back to the android. "You look so much like the Glenda unit."

"Cosmetic parts from older units were used in manufacturing the Class-5 Series," she said.

"How is your generation different?"

"Prior generations were created for the purpose of reproduction. They were designed to replicate human beings physically and emotionally."

"Were you not designed the same?"

"The Class-5s were created without a limbic system in order to accommodate the installation of superior cortex drives. We are not programmed to replicate human emotional response."

Stanford paused. "What is your programming?"

"We were designed for the Project."

"Will you tell me about the Project?"

She shook her head.

There was silence inside the escort vehicle. The only sound came from the thrusters as they pivoted to navigate the dunes. Stanford's conversation with the Winifred unit seemed so private that he wondered if the other mutants had fallen asleep. For a brief moment he experienced a rush of anxiety as he realized that he was not unlike the android. His emotions were as non-functional as hers.

"What was that place back there?" he asked.

"That was a transfer station," said Winifred.

"A transfer to where?"

"I am not authorized to speak further on this topic." The android's pupils were miniscule inside her brown irises. "What are you going to do to me?"

"You didn't seem concerned about dying back at the transfer station. Do you care what happens to you?"

"Every organism, whether organic or synthetic, is hard-wired to fight for survival. But I knew you would not kill me."

"How did you know?"

"If you harm me, it will inevitably hurt us both."

"Hurt us how?"

Stanford looked into Winifred's eyes. Even now, he could not detect an ounce of humanity. She was right when she said that Class-5s were different from the previous generations of androids. Besides the genuine exoskeleton of tissue, she was almost pure machine.

"I won't harm you," he said. "But you need to tell me what I want to know or I can't promise your safety."

"If I continue this conversation, I will be killed by my creators."

The copper in Stanford's eyes began to swirl and glow.

"Your eyes are unusual," said Winifred.

"You are a woman of science. Tell me what's happening to me."

The android watched him closely. "It is a rare mutation."

"Am I the only one?"

"As I have stated, I am not at liberty to continue this conversation."

"Tell me what you are doing to those people at the transfer station."

The android closed her eyes, ending the conversation.

From the front of the vehicle came the voice of the assassin. "We are nearing the base, men. Good work out there tonight. Let's unpack and get some rest."

Stanford felt the military vehicle slowing as it reached the outskirts of the rebel camp. Out the windshield he could see the cluster of tents; and in the distance, beyond the encampment, was the outline of the Salus dome. The top of the crown was lit from within, causing the entire structure to glow faintly in the night.

The shape was as foreboding as the first time he laid eyes on it. He recalled standing in the penthouse of the Central Tower, staring down upon the quadrant in search of the dome, doubting its very existence. The search was over now. He knew it was only a matter of time before he would come face to face with the sanctuary, with no way in but by force.

He looked back at the android. "You've been inside Salus?"

She kept her eyes closed, without a word.

2.16
AN ELECTRIC DREAM

Stanford stared out at the Perfect colony through the curved windows of the viewing room on the top floor of the Central Tower. From way up high he could see the wall separating the mutants to the west and the outer boundaries to the north, but he could not see Salus.

A brilliant mushroom cloud exploded in the quadrant below, rising like a fiery inferno. The explosion sparkled in the viewing room, breaking into hues of primary colors.

He adjusted his double-tinted glasses and watched the ashen cloud dissipate into the atmosphere. He thought about how awe-inspiring the explosion was, like a flower blooming in the night sky. In the very heart of the devastation was something beautiful, something alive.

From behind, he felt the gentle touch of arms wrap around his waist.

A soft voice tickled his ear. "Can you see Salus?"

Stanford looked more carefully at the metropolis below, scanning all the way to the empty desert. "No."

"Look to the north. Take off your glasses."

Stanford complied, but he could not detect the dome. "It's not there. Does Salus exist?"

He saw an owl streak across his line of vision, flapping its broad wings until it disappeared from view. He thought about the freedom of being able to fly from one colony to the other, crossing over the wall like it was no impediment at all. The birds were the only living things on Ultim that had retained their free will. The owl was the second image of beauty that he had seen through the windows of the viewing room.

The voice spoke again from behind. "Come with me, Stanford. Let me show you something."

Stanford turned to see the woman walking away, her hips swaying as if to soft music; dark hair bouncing in the bun atop her head.

They exited through a rear door and came to the therapy room, furnished with comfortable couches. The sound of a waterfall was piped in from the overhead speakers.

The woman turned toward him, revealing herself. Her skin was pale and flawless, her lips painted with vibrant red lipstick.

He resisted the urge to approach her. She was the third beautiful image he had seen since entering the viewing room.

"Do you remember coming here before?" she asked.

"Yes."

"What do you remember about it?"

"I remember the fern."

The woman smiled. "Go to it."

Stanford craned his head toward a display case covered by a curtain.

"Go on," said the woman. "Don't be shy."

He hesitated, reluctant to meet the fern again. It had brought him so much pleasure—but had also taken so much away. It was an unpredictable relationship. But the urge was too much to resist. He walked slowly to the case and drew back the curtain.

The case was empty.

He looked back at the woman. He felt both hurt and relieved. "Where did it go?"

The woman sat on the couch and loosened her bun. Her hair fell upon her shoulders like woven silk.

Stanford felt a warm sensation creeping into his loins.

"The Patron took it." Her voice was suddenly flat.

Stanford hesitated. "But the Patron gave it to the Director as a gift."

"Oh, Stanford, you are such a ninny. Everything belongs to the Patron—don't you know that by now?" The woman hiked her dress up to expose her silky smooth thighs.

"What are you doing?"

"Stanford, don't you know when a woman is trying to seduce you?"

Stanford took a step forward.

"Make love to me, Mr. Samuels."

Stanford crossed the therapy room and sat down on the couch next to her. He took her into an embrace, placing his lips against hers. He watched her pupils constrict to the size of pinpricks.

He pulled back. "Are you an android, Ilsa K?"

The woman smiled. "Stanford, I told you not to be a ninny. My name is Winifred."

The android grew impatient. She moved quickly, straddling him and pulling open his panda jacket, running her hands along his chest.

He tried to speak, but she pressed her mouth against his. He felt the leverage of her body slowly forcing him into a supine position. Before he knew it, she was on top of him.

She unbuttoned her blouse, exposing the mounds of her perfectly tear-shaped breasts.

Stanford reached to touch her, but she grabbed his wrists and pinned his arms by his sides.

The android was sitting directly on Stanford's diaphragm. He struggled to catch his breath.

"You told me you couldn't feel emotion," he said.

Winifred was breathing heavily. "Emotion and pleasure are not one and the same. Now you will experience that for yourself."

"Experience what?"

"This will be the first time you've made love since being transformed into an android, Mr. Samuels."

Stanford struggled beneath her. "I'm not—"

Winifred smiled. "You need me."

He could not overcome her strength. He felt her hips rocking rhythmically on top of him. There was no way to contain the fire burning in his loins.

He allowed the android to devour him.

The sounds of the waterfall flowed gently overhead.

2.17
WAKE-UP CALL

Stanford's eyes took a moment to come into focus. When his vision clarified, he saw the assassin sitting on the floor of the tent, warming a pot of coffee over the fire.

The assassin noticed him. "You're awake."

Stanford propped himself up on his elbow. His head felt thick.

"You talk a lot in your dreams," said the assassin. "Did you know that?"

"How would I know that?"

The assassin took the pot off the fire and poured the steaming coffee into a mug. He handed it to Stanford. "You sound like you could use some."

Stanford accepted the cup and took a sip. The liquid warmed his throat.

"Dreams are the only place we can escape," said the assassin. "There are no boundaries to our imaginations. No walls or domes keeping us out. We can go anywhere we want, as long as we can dream it."

"But it's a trick," said Stanford. "The walls are back as soon as we wake up."

The assassin nodded and sipped his coffee. "It seems cruel, doesn't it? But there are ways of walking through the walls even when you're awake."

"What do you mean?"

The assassin fetched a leather pouch that lay on the ground behind him. He pulled out a feathery fern frond. "Have you ever heard of a daytime hallucination, Stanford? These ferns have some amazing properties. They not only heal, but they offer a temporary relief from reality. You might say they bestow the gift of second sight. One only has to ingest a small sample to achieve a waking dream."

Stanford sat fully upright. "Why would you want to fool yourself by blurring reality?"

The assassin chuckled. "That's just it, Stanford. The experience is completely lucid—more lucid than reality, in fact. You can perceive things that you would not normally notice. It heightens the senses. You can smell things that would normally escape you; hear frequencies that you've never heard before; feel textures in perfectly ordinary objects that you never knew existed. Why don't you give it a try and experience it first hand?"

"You've already been inside my head more often than I'm comfortable with, Mr. Dekkar."

"Oh come now, Stanford. If you've seen me in your visions, then I was entirely of your creation. You willed me to be there. You are the master of your own fantasies."

"Either way, I've had enough fern for now."

"Very well. But keep it in mind," said the assassin. "It's relaxing and enlightening at the same time. In proper doses, it's pleasurable. The only problem is that it can be addictive, so we need to exercise caution."

Stanford stood up and brushed the sand off his pants. "Thanks for the warning. Do you mind if I borrow your mug?"

"Yes, of course." The assassin passed his mug across the fire. "Where are you headed, Mr. Samuels?"

"I've missed a few coffee breaks with my old friend. We need to catch up."

The assassin got to his feet. "Before you go, I should get you up to speed on the android. The EEG shows unusual brainwave activity. There are small pockets of intense activity but an overall lack of functions. My men are still reviewing the results and should know more soon. She's military, Stanford. That's the only way to explain the cloaking mechanism that hides her body heat. I can feel it in my bones."

"Where is she now?"

"We have her in a holding cell. She's perfectly comfortable, so don't worry about that. She's trying to bargain. She's willing to provide information in exchange for her release."

"Information about Salus?"

"I don't know. She says she'll only talk to you."

Stanford made his way toward the flap in the tent. He heard the assassin from behind.

"Oh, and Stanford?"

Stanford stopped to look back, seeing the assassin's wide grin.

"I'm flattered that you dream about me."

Stanford exited.

The assassin's laughter followed him out.

2.18
IRON MAN

As Stanford made his way to the infirmary, he heard the howls of the wild children coming from the darkness outside the base camp. He turned on his high beams and scanned the desert, but it was empty as far as he could see. The children were lost amongst the shadows, calling for help, but there was nothing he could do to comfort them. He hoped they would take care of each other.

He pushed through the flap of the medical tent and dimmed his eyes so as not to disturb the convalescing patients. Inside, he saw multiple cots arranged in aisles, much like how they appeared in the enemy compound. He paused to remember the location of his friend's cot and then walked up with two mugs of hot coffee.

He set the mugs on the sandy floor and gently shook the old man's shoulder. The color had not returned to his friend's face. He looked as gaunt and pale as he had back at the transfer station.

"Wake up, Iron Man. Can you hear me?"

The man was motionless. Stanford placed his hand on his friend's chest, feeling the faint beats of an old drum.

"If you were awake right now, you'd probably scold me for leaving my old life, just like you scolded me so many

120

times in the past for my poor decisions. You were like a father to me. I don't know how I could have gotten on without you."

Stanford stared deeply at the man, watching for a sign that his words might be filtering through.

"I wish I could explain my decision to you, but the truth is I don't want to contemplate it anymore. I don't have the capacity to regret things that happened before now. It may sound strange, but I've come to realize that it's better that way. The pain is gone."

The man's hand twitched ever so slightly. A blip of vitality had returned to his body.

Stanford continued. "But just because I can't feel the past, doesn't mean I can't remember it. I know what you did for me, and I want to repay you by making you feel as comfortable as I possibly can. Open your eyes and have a coffee with me again, Iron Man. Wake up . . ."

Stanford watched the old man's eyes slowly part to take him in.

"Saturn, is that you?" The man's words fluttered on weak breath.

"Yes, Iron Man, it's me."

Stanford could see confusion flickering behind the old man's eyes. He placed his hand on his friend's chest, feeling the slow labored breaths that fought desperately to escape the taxed lungs.

"Are you uncomfortable?"

The man nodded.

"Where does it hurt?"

The man winced as he placed his hand gently on his lower abdomen.

"I will get you something for the pain. Can you tell me what happened to you?"

There was a long pause.

"Tell me what you remember, Iron Man."

"I remember going for a walk." His voice was barely audible.

"What happened after you went for a walk?"

"There was a truck . . ." His voice trailed off.

"Who was in the truck? What kind of truck?"

"I don't . . ."

The old man's voice petered out. An instant calm washed over his body. His facial features relaxed as he achieved a moment of peace. "I'm so tired, Saturn."

Stanford gripped his friend's hand. "I brought you a coffee, Iron Man. Let's just sip our coffee like we used to. We don't have to talk."

His friend was unresponsive. He had slipped back into the coma from which he had come.

Stanford felt for a heartbeat. It was weak but still present.

He stared down at the mugs on the sandy floor.

I have nothing else to give you, God. I have no reason to believe that you are a just and righteous God, for you have never shown yourself to me. But if you are what others claim you are, then spare this man. He has suffered all his life. Please allow him to go on his own terms, in peace. I ask so little of you. You have done even less for me.

The man was perfectly still on the cot. His eyes remained closed.

Stanford leaned over to pick up the mugs, tipping one over into the sand. The liquid formed a small pool at his feet, steaming like a hot spring; then slowly seeped into the sandy floor.

"Are you okay, Mr. Samuels?" The voice belonged to a female.

Stanford's eyes blazed like the twin suns as he craned his neck toward the flap of the tent. "He's not well."

"He'll be treated with the fern," said the resident mother. "The medics will perform a full evaluation. Your eyes are on fire."

"I've been able to control them since the cleansing, but there are still times they ignite on their own."

The mother approached. "You are hurting, Mr. Samuels. Even though you've been cleansed, there is still some residual pain inside you. It seeps out through your eyes. This man meant a lot to you."

Stanford nodded.

"What can I do for you?" asked the mother.

Stanford stared at the overturned mug and listened to the howls echoing through the night. "The children are crying," he said.

"They have each other, Mr. Samuels; just like we have each other. There is strength in packs. We have to stick together in order to accomplish our mission. We could not do it on our own."

Stanford dimmed his eyes and looked into the mother's warm face. Her skin had been licked by the cruel tongue of radiation, yet she maintained a quiet dignity. She smiled at him through the darkness of the tent.

Stanford admired her strength, wishing for an ounce of her power to transfer into him. It was almost impossible to imagine how a woman who had experienced so many traumas could continue to exude such a degree of maternal affection. She must be a guardian angel for the Tech Terrorists, he thought.

He watched as she stooped to pick the coffee mugs off the sandy floor. Now he could look into her clear blue eyes at close range. The eyes were pure, untouched by radiation, revealing her gentle soul. He couldn't help but wonder how much she had left to give.

"Even if we find my child," he said, "what kind of life can I provide? He is without his mother."

"If you choose to accept us as your family, your child will be cared for in the residential tents. He will receive as much love from the surrogate mothers as is humanly possible. None of us can replace your wife, Mr. Samuels, but I would consider it a great honor to care for your child, as if he was my own blood. All of the mothers here can offer a loving bond, not just for him, but for you. How else do you think we've survived out here so long? Human beings are not designed to be alone. We nurture and support one another. You'll see. And like every family, there will be squabbles. It's what makes the experience so authentic."

Stanford smiled. "Thank you, Mother."

She nodded. "Don't look at me with sympathy. This is where I belong. I am happy to be with my people."

Stanford watched the mother exit the tent, replaced by the figure of the assassin.

Howls filled the night once again.

"The pack of wild children is moving closer, Mr. Samuels," said the assassin.

Stanford nodded. The copper swirled in his pupils like an apocalyptic storm.

"Are you okay, Stanford?"

Stanford looked directly at the assassin. "Mr. Dekkar, it's time you take me to the android."

2.19
THE HOWLING

The assassin led Stanford across the encampment. Out of the corners of his eyes, Stanford caught flashes of children scampering on all fours along the edge of the base. The creatures shot in and out of the shadows like stalking predators. They were moving in.

"They're circling the camp," said the assassin.

Stanford shot his head around, following their movements. "Maybe they're hungry. We should feed them."

The assassin halted his advance. "You want to give our food rations to a pack of wild dogs?"

"They aren't dogs, Mr. Dekkar."

"We have a limited supply. We can't just toss our rations in the desert for scavengers."

"How else will we know if they are hungry?"

The assassin shrugged. "Okay, Mr. Samuels." He fished in his cargo pants, retrieving a food bar in a plastic wrapper. "This is pure energy protein. We give it to all the troops before battle. Let's put your theory to the test."

The assassin peeled the wrapper and tossed the offering into the boundary. In less than a minute, a child appeared out of the darkness, crawling cautiously along the sand toward the food. He sniffed and prodded it with a finger before looking directly into Stanford's glowing eyes. The child was still for a moment, then bared its teeth and lurched forward.

The assassin drew his pistol.

"Don't shoot," said Stanford. "He won't come near us."

"How do you know?"

"He's posturing."

Stanford took a step toward the boy and immediately the child back-pedaled.

"What are you doing?" asked the assassin. There was an edge of nervousness in his voice.

Stanford took another step forward. This time the child turned and ran off into the night.

"I guess he doesn't like energy bars," said the assassin. "I don't much like them myself."

"He would have eaten it if he was hungry."

"So why are they here?"

Stanford looked at the assassin. "You've been out in the desert for longer than I have. Why don't you tell me?"

"In all my time in the outer boundaries, I had never encountered a wild child until recently, nor had I heard of one. I don't know what they are or where they came from. This is new to me, Stanford."

The men continued toward the tent. The sound of howling seemed to come from all directions.

"I think they are coming to collect their friend," said Stanford.

Another howl echoed through the night, but this time it was closer. It came from within the base.

The assassin drew his weapon and spun around to face the tent where the imprisoned wild child was being held.

They quickly crossed the sand and pushed through the flap. From inside the cage came the sounds of weeping.

Stanford illuminated the small naked child inside. The boy was gripping the bars, his entire body trembling. His clothes had been discarded in a pile in the corner. Tears flooded out of his wide, terrified eyes.

Stanford turned to the assassin. "Where are the keys, Mr. Dekkar?"

"What are you doing, Stanford?"

"Those children out there—they've come to reunite their family."

"You don't know what you're talking about, Mr. Samuels. You are guessing."

The child in the cage emitted a piercing howl.

The howling was returned from outside.

The boy rattled the cage in a desperate effort to get out.

"Give me the keys, Mr. Dekkar. I command you."

The assassin sighed as he reached into his cargo pants. "You've got some strange ideas, Mr. Samuels, but what do I know?" He handed over the keys.

As Stanford stepped toward the cage, the child retreated to the far side and flopped down in the sand. He pulled his legs up to his chest and began rocking back and forth, just like he had done before.

Stanford cracked open the door.

"You see?" said the assassin. "He's not even smart enough to sense his own freedom."

"He's self-soothing," said Stanford.

After a moment, the child lifted his head and glanced at the open door. Stanford took a step away.

The child slowly inched forward.

Stanford gestured for the assassin to step as far back as possible. They both watched in silence as the child exited the cage, his head darting back and forth to detect danger, and then shot out the flap of the tent as fast as he could.

They ran out after him, watching as he scuttled across the base on all fours, kicking up sand in his wake. As soon as he reached the edge of the encampment, the sound of gunfire broke the night, and the child slumped to the ground as if he had been struck.

Stanford whirled around, seeing Joshua with a cocked rifle.

Joshua looked back. "I got him, sir."

The copper swirled in Stanford's eyes like never before. He blasted his eye-beams on Joshua with such intensity that the mutant soldier dropped his rifle and shielded his face.

Stanford approached quickly and slammed his knuckles into the bridge of Joshua's nose.

Joshua collapsed to the sand and yelped. Blood spurted out both nostrils. "What the hell are you doing?" His voice gurgled from the blood filling his throat.

"You know nothing about Hell, Joshua. But if that boy dies, you'll get a fast education."

The assassin rushed up behind Stanford and tried to restrain him. "Stanford, please get under control. Joshua is only doing what he's been trained to do. He didn't know what was happening."

Stanford looked directly at the assassin. "Joshua is a liability to the mission, Mr. Dekkar. Either you rectify the situation, or I will."

The assassin nodded. "I'll take care of it, Mr. Samuels."

Stanford traversed the sand toward the wild child.

When he reached the edge of the base, he found the boy motionless, face down in the blood-soaked terrain. There was a gaping wound from a bullet hole in his back.

Howls pierced the night sky.

Stanford knelt down and carefully turned the boy over. He put his ear to his chest.

"He is still alive," he said. "Let's get him to the infirmary."

With the assassin's help, they carried the boy across the sand to the medical tent.

Joshua stayed where he was, crumpled and bleeding.

2.20
NURTURING

The room was filled with hundreds of incubators, all lined up in rows. They were capsule-shaped, with glass tops. The digital display on the sides of the cases showed random identification numbers.

Nurses in clean white scrubs walked up and down the aisles, opening each capsule to remove a newborn from within. The children were remarkably calm as the nurses rocked each of them for exactly one minute before placing their little bodies back in the capsule and moving on down the aisle.

On the other side of a one-way mirror was a waiting room where a head nurse watched on. Behind her, seated in a cluster of chairs, was a gathering of scientists, each wearing a lab coat bearing the acronym: PAD.

"The nurturing process is critical to the child's neurological development," said the head nurse. "Studies have shown that holding a child for precisely one minute, at least four times a day, directly increases social-emotional conditioning. Our nurses work around the clock, ensuring proper brain maturity and good physical health. The children will be cared for like this for the first two years of life and then downgraded to Step 2-care protocol for the following two years. It's a four year program leading to adoption."

One of the scientists raised his hand. "What's Step 2?"

The nurse smiled broadly. "During Step 2 we reduce the frequency of nurturing by half. We know that ninety percent of brain growth takes place in the first three years, but cutting down the nurturing from four to two times per day during years three and four yields no noticeable gaps in the child's development. In fact, data shows that the reduced frequency actually produces more confident, independent children."

Another scientist raised his hand. "Can you speak about your efficiency rate?"

The nurse's lips thinned. "That's a hard question with a complex answer that can be better addressed in another forum. What I can say is that in order to understand numbers, you must first recognize our brief history. It's imperative to realize that the nurturing program was not funded by the Patron until the fourth generation fertility bots were introduced into circulation. But I can assure you we have a sparkling success rate."

"But have you accumulated specific empirical data?"

"Yes, of course. All of our research is made available in the archive room. The project is transparent. If you would like to see more, I can speak to you after. But, as I said, this is a more general session."

Another scientist spoke. "How do you respond to rumors that uncivilized children were released into the outer boundaries?"

The nurse paused. "The rumors of children being released from our facility are completely false and, quite frankly, offensive. We do everything in our power to care for each and every child as if they are our own offspring. We made mistakes in the past, of course, but the reality is the facility was stretched to its limits by the influx of children from the fertility bots. We did the best we could with the limited resources granted to our pioneer program. We would never hide our faults, and certainly not abandon the children under our care. Many of our nurses were never selected as Eradicators, and this is their only chance to be caregivers. Even though these children are spawned by androids, our staff has adopted them as their own. This isn't just a job. This is a way of life, and we all take it very seriously. No child has been abandoned. I promise you that."

"What about the special boy?" asked the first scientist. "Do you keep him in the general population?"

"No," said the nurse. "Capsule 40065 is in quarantine under the Patron's orders."

"Can you tell us why?"

"The boy is unique. Beyond that, you'd have to ask the Patron himself."

"Will the Patron be available for comment?"

There was a chuckle amongst the scientists.

"He's rather busy," said the nurse, feigning a smile.

"Can you take us to the quarantine?"

The nurse scanned the men in the chairs. "As a matter of fact, I can. I'm the head of the nurturing unit; I have authorization. Follow me," she said.

The collection of scientists exited the lobby and followed the nurse down a hallway to the rear of the facility. The quarantine room was fortified by steel doors with a serpentine camera.

The camera extended on a flexible neck.

"Requesting access to capsule 40065," said the nurse.

The camera investigated her body like a curious snake before retracting to the hole above the door. Moments later, the steel vault opened automatically.

The quarantine room was small, forcing the scientists to pack tightly inside.

At the room's center was a single incubation capsule.

"This is patient 40065," said the nurse.

The scientists jostled to get a closer look at the child sleeping soundlessly inside.

"He looks the same as the others," said a scientist. "Why is this one so interesting to the Patron?"

The nurse stepped toward the capsule. "Patient 40065 has a rare but spectacular mutation. The key to his eradication could very well be a breakthrough for modern genetic research."

"Can you show us the mutation?"

The nurse glanced through the enclosure at the sleeping child. The boy inside was completely at peace. She began to tap on the glass. "Wake up, boy. You have guests. Wake up . . . wake up."

The child began to stir.

The nurse continued to tap until the tiny newborn finally opened his mutant eyes, flooding the interior of the incubator with brilliant light.

The scientists closest to the capsule shielded their eyes from the glare.

The nurse smiled. "Gentlemen, allow me to introduce you to child number 40065."

2.21
FAMILY

The assassin poured the fern concoction down the back of the wild child's throat. "All we can do is wait, Stanford."

Stanford stared down at the boy lying unconscious on the cot. This was not a wild creature, defined by howls and canines. This was a boy in need of help; a vulnerable human child who had lost his way in the dark and needed to find his way home. Stanford wanted to take the boy's hand and lead him to safety. But for now he could only stand by and hope the fern would bring him back, much like it had done for him. Stanford felt helpless.

"I wish I could go to him," he said softly.

"Go to whom, Stanford—the wild or your own son?"

Stanford looked into the child's face and envisioned the face of his son. He wanted desperately to reach out and touch him.

"Bring me a frond," said Stanford.

"Excuse me?"

"I want to bring him back."

"Bring him back from where, Mr. Samuels? Let the fern do its thing. We have other business to take care of. The android is waiting in the interrogation tent. We have to plan for Salus."

Stanford felt his eyes growing hot. "I know what we need to do, Mr. Dekkar. Bring me a frond."

The assassin fetched his leather pouch and removed a feathery leaf. "You're the boss, Mr. Samuels. How would you like it prepared, steeped or steamed?"

"I'll take it raw."

The assassin handed over the fern and watched Stanford put the entire leafy green in his mouth.

"The raw preparation is the most potent, Stanford. There's no gauging the level of toxicity you are about to ingest."

When Stanford had consumed the fern, he wiped his mouth and smiled. "Maybe I'll see you in my dreams, Mr. Dekkar."

The assassin attempted to smile back, but he couldn't fake it. His expression was one of concern. "Good luck, Stanford. Whatever happens, find your way back."

Stanford nodded and lay on an empty cot next to the wild child. He closed his eyes and listened to the sounds of howling outside the tent. The sound pierced his ears, and he felt a shooting pain through his temples. He sat up with a start and looked around at the empty tent. He was alone now. The other cots had vanished. The assassin was no longer standing over him.

He swung his legs over the side of the bed and walked out of the tent into wide open desert. The entire encampment had vanished. He looked in all directions and saw nothing but lonely sand dunes. The Salus dome that once glowed in the distance was no longer there. It was as if he had been transported to a deserted moon. His breath condensed in the crisp air, and he felt a shiver run through his body.

He didn't know where to walk first, so he walked straight forward. He was careful with his footfalls on the uneven terrain. When he looked back, the infirmary tent was gone. He felt utterly alone in the pitch black desert. Every living thing had been swallowed up by the dark.

He squeezed his hands into tight fists, attempting to control his eyes. He felt the tension pulse through his body until his irises activated a bright path before him. Up ahead, he saw the old boy wagging his tail.

The dog barked excitedly and ran out of the range of his eye-beams.

"Wait for me, old boy!"

Stanford ran after the collie, losing his footing and falling face down in the sand. Beneath his body he felt something hidden below the surface. He brushed off a layer of sand to reveal a section of metallic track. The fusion train had passed by there, its path now covered over by a thick layer of dust and ash. He heard the dog barking up ahead, beckoning him. He struggled to his feet and continued his pursuit.

"Where are you going, old boy? I can't see you. Don't leave me."

But I left him.

Stanford continued forward. His lungs began to sting in his chest. He slowed his pace to conserve energy and listened for his companion.

"Are you there, old boy? Come back, please."

As he advanced carefully across the sand, he heard the sound of barking again. He felt an instant burst of adrenaline and forged ahead on tired legs. "I can't see you, old boy. Where are you?"

Soon the barking transformed into the howls of wild dogs. At the furthest range of his eye-beams, he could see a forest of tall ferns sprouting up from the desert floor; the tallest of the fronds stretching into the sky like great majestic fir trees. He saw the collie weaving amongst the stalks.

"Sit, old boy. Stay there."

Stanford charged forward but the dog disappeared into the thicket. The howling of the wild animals was louder than ever. He made the decision to enter the forest, moving as quickly as he could through the dense vegetation.

Navigating through the tall ferns, he came to a clearing with a shallow pool of still water. All around the perimeter of the pool were dozens of wild children. They scooped their hands in the water to drink. None of the children appeared to be beyond the age of five or six. They were unclothed, and he could see that there was an even mix of boys and girls.

They looked at him when he entered the clearing.

Stanford spotted the child who had been captive at the base. His body appeared to be healed. The child stared back with recognition and immediately bolted into the forest. The other wilds bared their teeth and snarled. Stanford ran after the child.

He stumbled through the thicket in pursuit. The forest was extremely dense, making it virtually impossible to move faster than a snail's pace. He felt his frustration mounting. His lungs were not cooperating. He collapsed in his place, trying to catch his breath.

Sitting there, Stanford saw a face poke through the fern stalks. It was the face of the child.

"Wait!" he shouted.

The face disappeared into the thicket.

Stanford got to his feet and ran as fast as he could, his vision obliterated by the vegetation, until he collided with a solid wall. He crumpled to the ground.

When he regained his senses, he saw that he had contacted the base of the Salus dome. The outer membrane was solid, similar in consistency to cement, but seemed to vibrate as if it was a living organism.

He could hear a hum coming from inside. The sound was unlike anything he had ever heard, but he imagined an electrical storm captured within. He stood up and approached the dome. The electricity sounded more intense with each step he took. When he was within arm's length, he stretched his hand toward the dome and placed his palm on the exterior. Despite its appearance, the texture of the wall was soft and malleable, and he felt like he could push right through.

His hand adhered to the wall like a suction cup, and within moments the dome had sucked his arm through to the other side. He felt a prickling sensation on his fingertips, and a current ran up his forearm, warming his body and making the hairs stand up on his neck.

The dome began to pulse as if it had a heartbeat.

Stanford felt completely at ease. The experience was pleasurable. He felt his eyelids growing heavy, and he wanted to lie down on the forest floor and fall asleep.

He suddenly felt a shock that sent him several feet backward into the thick ferns. From his landing place, he could no longer see the wall of the dome. The ferns had covered it over like a thick blanket of protection. He examined his hand, looking for scorch marks, but there were none. He could feel the last remnants of electricity exit his body, and then he felt the chill of night.

Out the corner of his eye, he saw the wild child's face poke through the stalks of ferns to regard him.

"Don't run away," said Stanford. He struggled to catch his breath. "I'm here to help you."

"How do you think you can help me, sir? You look like the one who needs saving. Besides, I'm with my family now. We may not be inside Salus, but we are together."

Stanford looked at the child's face. The grime and dirt had been washed away, uncovering a handsome young boy with strong cheek bones and soft, dark eyes.

"You can talk?"

"Of course I can talk," said the wild. "We all can. After years neglected in the nursery, we learned to communicate in our own way. Just because you don't understand us, doesn't mean we're uncivilized. You are ignorant."

"But you speak English."

"It only sounds like English when we are here. This place makes everything the same."

"This place isn't real," said Stanford. "I need to take you back so you can find your family in the real world. Your mother and father must be waiting for you inside Salus."

The boy snarled. "I live with the pack."

"What about your parents?"

"I don't have parents."

"You must have a mother."

"I was birthed by a synthetic. We all were. I would hardly call the android my mother."

"You are offspring of the Glenda bots?"

"Not Glenda. An earlier generation."

"There were androids capable of reproduction prior to Glenda?"

"Yes, but the PAD kept us hidden. When Salus was populated, the Patron cast us out, not wanting a reminder of his failure. Now we live amongst the ferns."

Stanford was quiet for a moment. "Come back with me. I can adopt you."

"Come back where? To my cage? I've spent my whole life in a cage."

"There will be no more cages," said Stanford. "I'll take care of you as if you were my own."

The boy grinned. "Are you using me to replace your son?"

"What do you know about my son?"

"Everybody who's been inside Salus knows about your son, Mr. Samuels."

"Have you seen him?"

"Nobody has seen him. But we know he's there. He's in quarantine. They say his incubator shines like the twin suns used to."

"I need to get my boy back," said Stanford. "Can you take me to him?"

The wild child smiled and reached out his hand. "Let me show you something."

Stanford followed the boy through the thicket. The sound of a waterfall was within earshot.

When they arrived at a wide clearing, Stanford could see a stream of blue-green water gushing over a high cliff, creating a frothy cascade in the pool below. On the far side, he saw his mother sitting on the bank, dangling her legs in the water.

Nearby, Stanford's father played fetch with the old boy.

Stanford let go of the wild child's hand and moved toward the pool. "Mom . . . Dad?"

His parents looked at him and smiled.

"Where are your glasses?" asked his mother.

"I don't need them anymore."

"What do you mean you don't need them anymore? You know how important it is to protect your eyes."

"I know, Mom. But I don't need them. I'm cured."

His mother smiled. Her eyes showed the mutant gene she carried, her irises swirling and glowing with copper rings. "Isn't that nice? I'm proud of you, sweetie."

His father smiled too. "I always knew it. You're no different than anybody else, son. You hear me?"

"Yes, Dad."

"He is different," said his mother. "He's a king."

"My son—the king." His father chuckled. "Why don't you cool off in the pool with us, Stanford? You're not still sore that we left you, are you?"

"It wasn't your fault. It was an accident."

"I wish we could have stayed with you longer," said his father.

"You couldn't control it," said Stanford.

He noticed his mother's brilliant eyes and felt an ache in his chest. He desperately wanted to lay his head on her lap—to feel her hand caressing his hair the way she used to when she put him to sleep at night all those years ago.

"You've grown into such a handsome young man," said his mother. "Come be with us, honey. Let us take the pain away."

"I can't. I have a son now."

His mother looked overjoyed. "Oh, Stanford, that's wonderful! What's his name?"

"I called him Sander."

"That's a beautiful name, honey. Sander Samuels."

His father glowed with pride. "Your mother and I look forward to meeting our grandchild. Bring him for a visit soon, okay?"

Stanford's vision was bleary. He watched the old boy bring the stick back to shore. The dog sat on the beach and wagged his tail like a metronome.

"We'll be here, Stanford," said his mother. "Whenever you're ready, we'll be waiting right here."

Stanford felt the wild child take his hand and lead him back toward the dense forest of ferns. Stanford didn't want to go, but soon the vision of his family was gone. The ferns grew up to fill what had been of the empty clearing.

"That's your family," said the child, "and I have a family of my own."

Tears leaked down Stanford's cheeks.

"I want to go home," said the boy. "But I don't want to go with you inside Salus."

Stanford squeezed the boy's hand. "I understand. Can we go back now?"

The child nodded.

Together, they disappeared into the thicket of ferns.

PART VI

BREACH

2.22
BABY ROOM

Audrey entered the bathroom with a flourish, staring at her brightly colored eye makeup in the vanity mirror. She spun around, seeing the condensation booth behind her, quickly opening the glass door to peek inside.

"My goodness, I can't get enough of the meditation lounger," she said to herself. "How is a modern woman expected to get anything done with such luxury beckoning to her all day? I could melt into the cushions and be perfectly content."

Audrey let the robe drop off her shoulders and stepped inside the booth, sitting in the chair.

"It's absolutely glorious," she said, reaching to depress a button on the nearby shower console. In an instant, soothing melodies floated down from a hidden speaker while a warm, detoxifying mist rained upon her face.

Audrey emitted an exaggerated moan. "It's like an expensive salon. I'm so pampered. But I mustn't be such a sloth. William will be home soon and I must appear busy."

Audrey jumped from the seat and exited the condensation booth in a hurry. She donned the robe once again, cinching the belt as she made her way to the master bedroom. Standing in front of the dresser mirror, she took a moment to blot her damp cheeks and fix her makeup, which had smeared under the mist, before changing into a floral pattern wraparound dress. The dress brought a smile to her face. When she was adequately done up, she fetched the feather duster and crossed the hall to a smaller room with powder blue walls and false sunshine filtering through the window. In the center was a crib with a virtual mobile hanging over the top.

Audrey instinctively rubbed her belly. "This room is perfect for you, Baby Andrew," she said. "I can't wait for you to see it."

She set the feather duster to the side and approached the crib, absently spinning the mobile as though she were stuck in a daydream.

The mobile was constructed of a grouping of interconnected icons suspended in midair, depicting six wild animals that existed inside Salus. There was an icon showing the head of an eagle, another of a cobra; also an owl, a lion, a moose, and a brown bear. As the mobile spun in a circle, it began to glow and envelop the crib in a comfortable pocket of white light.

"It's a sleep arc," she whispered, as if to an imaginary child in the crib. "I wonder if we can get one installed in the master bedroom to cure William's insomnia. I'm sure he won't mind the design. After all, he's a child at heart."

She smiled to herself before randomly pressing the icon that represented the eagle.

An image was suddenly projected on the far wall.

Audrey turned to watch an eagle in full flight, soaring over the pristine surface of a glacial lake. The majestic bird extended its massive wings to full capacity, catching a gentle breeze and gliding effortlessly until its talons clutched the highest branch of a tall fir tree. In the far distance was the glorious backdrop of jagged mountaintops.

The voice of the Patron came from a virtual speaker embedded in the mobile.

"The eagle was one of the first to be set free inside Salus. It depicts the virtues that we all cherish. There is ferocity inside the bird, as well as determination and grace. The eagle is a predator, but respectful of its fellow mates in the animal kingdom. When the bald eagle soars to great heights, you can think of freedom and bliss. You too can dream of grand achievements. Let the image of the eagle inspire you, young child. Let the beautiful scenery soothe you . . . now kindly select another icon."

Audrey pondered while allowing her eyes to glance between the floating icons, but her train of thought was interrupted by the sound of the door opening in the down-stairs foyer. The mobile became an afterthought as she rushed down the staircase. "William," she said. "Welcome home, darling."

The man entered the living room holding a recently dead fish.

Audrey stopped in her tracks at the sight of it. "William, what is that?"

"It's a rainbow trout, dear. I brought it for dinner. Aren't you proud of me?"

Audrey scrunched her nose. "It smells foul, honey. Where did you get it?"

"It smells perfectly natural," said William. "I caught it this morning. It is ready for skinning."

Audrey stared at the protruding eyes of the trout in silence.

"What's the matter?" asked her husband.

Audrey hesitated. "Nothing is the matter, darling. I don't think you meant skinning. I think what you meant to say is that I need to fillet the fish."

William laughed as he entered the kitchen and deposited the fish on the countertop. "Quite right," he said. "I'm so happy to have married such an intelligent woman." He turned around to place his gentle hand on her midriff.

"You have fish hands, William," she said, flinching.

"I'm sorry," he said. "I'll go wash up. How much time do I have till Michael arrives?"

"They said he'd be here by now, William. I'm nervous."

"Oh, Audrey, you know how you get. You're a ball of nerves."

"Don't tease me, William."

"I'm sorry, honey." He leaned in to kiss her.

"You smell like the sea."

William laughed. "I was on a lake!"

"The scent is unpleasant," said Audrey, "like you were marooned for a week."

William continued to chuckle as he ascended the staircase. "It's a brilliant setting," he said. "You can't imagine such gorgeous scenery. I hope I can convince you to leave your house chores to join me one day."

"Yes, yes, William, but there's just so much to do around here. And you know how low my energy is now that I'm packing around so much extra weight."

As soon as he reached the top of the stairs, the doorbell rang.

Audrey moved quickly to answer.

On the other side was a man wearing a blue uniform

with the PAD stitched to his breast pocket. A young boy with neatly-trimmed brown hair stood at his side.

"Are you Audrey Hampton?" asked the man.

"Yes."

"Is Michael Hampton your eradicated offspring?"

Audrey looked the boy from head to foot, holding back tears. "Yes," she said. "Do you need our official registration?"

The man waved his hand dismissively. "No. Have a nice day," he said, walking back toward the street.

William scampered down the staircase to meet his son. "Michael, my boy, please come in."

The boy entered with a very straight back. "Thank you for your hospitality."

Audrey glanced at her husband and then back at her boy. "No need to be so formal, Michael. It's just us."

"He's nervous, is all," said William. "Give the boy time."

Michael glanced between his parents.

"Oh my gosh," said Audrey. "You've gotten so big!" She pulled the child into an embrace. "Please come in and see your new home! It's really splendid. Your bedroom is absolutely wonderful."

The boy entered the kitchen, seeing the newly killed fish on the countertop. He glanced around at the surroundings. "What a wonderful living space. Have you been here long?"

Audrey shot her husband an uneasy look. "Michael, do you know where you are?"

Michael smiled broadly. "Of course I do. I am in the home of my creators."

"Don't call me your creator, Michael. I'm your mother."

William spoke up. "Son, whatever the boarding school taught you about proper etiquette is valuable, without question, but you can be yourself when you are here. This is your home. We want you to be comfortable."

Michael nodded his head sharply. "Yes, Father. I appreciate that. Where shall I bunk?"

Audrey emitted a tiny squeal of excitement. "Follow me to your new bedroom. You're sure to love it!"

The child followed his mother's bouncing figure up the staircase while William glanced proudly at the dead fish.

2.23
AWAKENING

When Stanford opened his eyes he saw the assassin staring down from above.

"Welcome back, Mr. Samuels."

Stanford felt a dull ache aggravating his temples. His vision took a moment to focus.

"How are you feeling?"

Stanford leaned over the side of the cot and vomited on the sandy floor.

"Don't feel the need to answer," said the assassin. "You need rest."

Stanford lay heavily back on the cot and turned his neck to the side, seeing the wild child sleeping soundlessly in the bed next to him. He tried to focus his eyes on the peaked ceiling of the tent while his vision swirled in a nauseating whirlpool. "It feels like my head is inside out."

"Your body is expelling toxins," said the assassin. "You've been sweating chlorophyll from your pores for several hours. It's a wonder you are lucid."

"How long was I out?"

"You need to rest, Mr. Samuels. I'll tell you everything when you're ready."

Stanford struggled to sit up, noticing the green-stained sheets that stuck to his sweaty torso. "Tell me." he said, before collapsing back on the cot.

The assassin placed a hand on Stanford's shoulder. "You need to get your strength up, Stanford. Give it another day and I'll tell you all you need to know."

"The boy," said Stanford. "Is he going to be okay?"

The assassin nodded. "He came through, Stanford. You brought him back."

"I was inside Salus."

"What did it look like?"

"I don't know. I could only get my arm inside. It felt like a static charge."

"Did it hurt?"

"No."

"Remember I told you the hallucinations heighten the senses. Your sense of touch was amplified by the fern." The assassin hesitated.

Stanford could see the secrets fluttering behind the mutant's eyes. All the years of training had placed the assassin's thoughts inside a steel vault, but Stanford's eyes penetrated the walls.

"What is it?" asked Stanford. "What's wrong?"

The assassin stared silently for another moment and then removed a portable video device from his cargo pants. He aimed the display screen at Stanford.

On screen, Stanford watched a point-of-view image from a land drone as it scooted across the sandy terrain toward Salus. As soon as the drone was within two hundred yards, the transmission cut out.

"We moved several drones into the airspace over Salus shortly after we lost signal from the ground."

The images on the screen showed a military assault on the Salus dome. Specialized artillery was launched from unmanned aircraft, completely ineffective against the protective shell. The dome sparkled brightly in the night where the bombs made contact. The outer membrane seemed to pulse as it was attacked, as if it thrived on the assault, growing stronger and more alive with each impact.

The video screen went dark when the transmission ended.

Stanford stared at the assassin. "What did you do?"

"You were out for nearly fourteen hours, Stanford. We couldn't wait."

"Wait for what?"

"We received intel while you were unconscious. We had to act on it."

"Who made the decision?"

"I did," said the assassin.

"And you stand by it?"

"Yes."

"What was the intel?"

"Stanford, why don't you rest and we can talk about this later?"

Stanford sat bolt upright. "Tell me now, Mr. Dekkar."

"We interrogated the Winifred unit, Stanford." The assassin paused. "They were sterilizing the solitaries."

"Which solitaries?"

"The ones at the transfer station."

"Iron Man?"

The assassin nodded.

"Why?"

"We're still collecting information."

Stanford exhaled deeply. His head had not settled. "What did you do to the android?"

"This is war, Stanford. We did what we had to."

Stanford felt the energy seep out of his body. He lay back down on the cot. The image of the glowing dome of Salus was prominent in his mind. "I wish you wouldn't have attacked Salus."

"We're running out of time, Mr. Samuels. We hit it with strategically placed doorway bombs designed to seek out vulnerabilities. Any weakness in the structure, whether it's a loose panel, or a seam, could point to a way in. We have to consider all options, unless you'd like to volunteer to knock on the front door."

"And did you detect vulnerabilities?"

The assassin shook his head. "Maybe you could take them a bottle of wine." He cracked a grim smile.

"You fired the first volley, Mr. Dekkar. They know we're coming."

The assassin held his gaze. "They always knew."

2.24
INTERROGATION

The android was slumped on the floor of a cage in the center of the interrogation tent, similar to the cage that had contained the wild child. Her white medical coat had been replaced by a tattered and filthy nightgown; her hair a tangled mess, completely obscuring the features of her face.

Joshua and another mutant were seated at a fold-up table nearby, laughing and pressing a button on a console. Each time the button was depressed, the android's entire body went into a state of violent convulsion.

"What is this?" asked Stanford, quickly approaching the soldiers.

Joshua and his partner appeared startled. They had been so mesmerized by the act of torture that they failed to notice the arrival of their superiors.

Joshua stood up, raising his hands to defend his swollen face.

"I demand to know what's happening here," said Stanford.

The assassin was near the flap of the tent. "Joshua has been collecting information, Mr. Samuels. A lot has happened since you went to sleep."

Stanford glanced at the cage, seeing wisps of smoke emanating from the android's tormented body. One of her trembling hands was bare of flesh, the skin and fingernails having been peeled completely off to reveal the metallic digits.

He shot a glance at the assassin. "Is this how you collect information?"

"We do what it takes, Mr. Samuels. I know this is hard for you. You were not raised a soldier, but this is our reality."

Stanford squeezed his hands into tight fists. "I told you to put a leash on Joshua."

"Joshua was following my orders. Information is retrieved by any means necessary. I'm sorry it's not pleasant for you, but this was not Joshua's call. It was mine."

"Where's the humanity, Mr. Dekkar?"

The assassin glanced between Joshua and his partner, both standing behind the desk as if they'd been afflicted by spontaneous rigor mortis. "You men are free to leave."

The men exited the tent quickly.

When they were gone, the assassin looked into Stanford's glowing eyes. "I know this is hard, Mr. Samuels, but humanity goes out the window when dealing with androids. She wasn't very cooperative at first, but the shock therapy seems to have opened her up. It's amazing how five thousand volts can spark even the most tight-lipped android."

Stanford looked at the girl in the cage. Her head was slumped on her chest, a mass of sweaty hair dangling over her face like an old mop.

The assassin walked over to the table and sat down in front of the console. "Winifred, I've brought somebody to see you."

The android trembled as the last currents of electricity escaped her body.

"There's nothing to be scared of now," said the assassin. "Mr. Samuels is here, as you requested."

Winifred slowly raised her head, revealing her pale, sticky complexion. Her lifeless eyes appeared sunken in her skull. "Fear is not in my programming."

"Maybe not," said the assassin. "But pain clearly is."

Stanford couldn't bear to listen to the interplay any longer. The android's suffering was too much to watch. "That's enough, Mr. Dekkar. Let her out of the cage."

The assassin snapped back. "I will do no such thing. She is a prisoner."

"I know what she is," said Stanford. "I can't have a conversation with her like this."

The assassin exhaled deeply as he fished in his cargo pants for the key. "Have it your way, Mr. Samuels." He glanced at the android.

Stanford scooped two empty chairs from behind the fold-up table and set them near the door of the cage. He sat down in one and gestured for the android to take the other.

Winifred moved cautiously out of her prison, keenly aware of the console that controlled the electricity. She sat in the seat opposite Stanford and caressed her damaged hand in her lap.

"I'm sorry you had to go through this," said Stanford.

Winifred gathered the strength to speak. "You humans spare no sorrow for androids."

"I don't like this any more than you do. If you cooperate, I promise you won't be hurt again."

"You shouldn't make promises you can't keep, Mr. Samuels."

"I can protect you."

"You should worry about yourself. You have no idea what's coming for you."

The assassin interjected. "Don't even think about making threats, Ms. Winifred."

The android held a steady gaze on Stanford. "What do you want to know?"

"I want to know where my son is."

"I told you before. I don't have the capacity for recall. No amount of torture can extract information that does not exist in my processor."

"But you've been inside Salus. You must know where they are keeping the incubators."

"I can only speak about details that pertain to my position in the Project."

"Fine, what can you tell me about the Project?"

"I know only about the surgeries."

"Are you sterilizing those people?" asked Stanford.

"Yes."

"Why?"

She paused again. "I don't know why, I only know my programming."

The assassin groaned with frustration, slamming his fist down on the console.

Instantly, the android began convulsing, gripping the arms of the chair. Her eyes rolled back in her head, exposing the stark whites.

Stanford shot around. "Stop it now, Mr. Dekkar!"

The assassin released the button. "I've warned her about playing coy, Mr. Samuels. She's repeating all the same information. I won't stand for it. She knows way more than she's saying."

When the surge ceased, the android slumped forward as the vitality exited her body in puffs of black smoke. Dark viscous fluid trickled out her ears and the corners of her mouth.

Stanford stood up from his chair and pulled Winifred's hair back into a ponytail, revealing the hidden electrodes attached to the sides of her skull. He peeled off the devices and tossed them on the sandy floor. "Mr. Dekkar, please leave the tent." The copper flecks swirled angrily in his eyes.

The assassin paused for a long moment, holding himself in check, before standing to leave. "I will be right outside if you need me, Mr. Samuels."

When Stanford sat back down, he took hold of the woman's metallic hand. It was cold without the fleshy insulation, so he placed his other hand over it in an attempt to warm her.

"Winifred, I can end your suffering."

He could feel the last remnants of the electrical current seeping from her fingertips, like vibrations moving along a guitar string.

She finally lifted her head. She had the appearance of a battered woman. "You can't send me back there. They will take me to the disassembling station."

"I'll protect you as long as I can. Tell me what's happening to the solitaries."

Her voice was weaker now, as if she knew she was sealing her fate with every word. "The Militia is collecting solitaries from the colony. They are being delivered to the transfer station for sterilization in preparation for Salus."

"Why?"

"I don't know. If I knew, I would tell you."

"If the solitaires are being transferred to Salus, then you must know a way inside."

"It is impossible to gain entrance, Mr. Samuels. Salus is protected by Class-5 soldiers."

"You said the Class-5s were created to be scientists."

"I said we were designed without limbic systems . . . without the ability to manufacture emotions . . . which is a desirable trait in scientists, and also in soldiers. They lack a conscience. Their sole purpose is to guard the dome and destroy anybody who poses a threat."

"How do we get past them?"

"There is no way, Mr. Samuels. They are more powerful than the Militia. The only way to stop them is to activate the shutdown feature in the PAD, but you can't get inside."

"There's a shutdown feature?"

"All intelligent androids have a unique verbal-activation shutdown command as a failsafe. Older units that pre-dated the mechanism were outfitted with aftermarket commands before being permitted inside Salus. Humans have never fully trusted that we wouldn't rise up and try to assume control. But the verbal feature is disabled in the soldiers. They can only be powered off by a global deactivation chip in their CPU, accessed through the central computer."

"Then we need to get inside the PAD."

"Your obsession has blinded you, Mr. Samuels. As soon as the Class-5s find out that the solitaries are missing from the transfer station, they will come looking for us. Your goal of Salus is a delusion."

"How long do we have?"

"The patients were in the recovery stage. The duration is twenty hours, which leaves you with approximately six hours remaining."

"I need you to go back in the cage, Winifred. Thank you for answering my questions."

Stanford closed the gate. "Are the solitaires aware they were sterilized?"

"It's a noninvasive radiosurgery. They may feel a sensation similar to indigestion, which passes quickly, but they have no recollection of the procedure."

Stanford made his way toward the exit.

The android called to him. "Mr. Samuels. Please don't send me back to the transfer station."

For a brief moment, Stanford wondered if there was a hint of fear in the android's eyes. He looked away and pushed through the flap without another word.

The assassin was standing nearby.

"Don't harm her again, Mr. Dekkar. We'll need her. Do you understand?"

The assassin nodded.

Stanford moved across the sand toward the residential tents.

2.25
A MEMORY

The infirmary tent was dark and silent. Stanford made his way up the aisle until he reached the cot where the Iron Man slept. He looked down at his friend, watching the slow, rhythmic pace of weary lungs. Standing over him, he was transported back to the mess hall at the factory. He remembered walking into the cafeteria for the first time, waves of anxiety sloshing in his stomach, squeezing his chest with such force he could barely breathe.

He navigated through the tables of mutants in search of a seat. What he wanted more than anything was a place of refuge—a place to escape the ceaseless chatter that bombarded him on all sides. He was a young man trying to adjust to his first day on the job, not to mention a new life. He recalled the overwhelming sensation of nervousness and self-doubt that attacked him. He felt alone, scared, desperate for a womb of protection to keep him safe.

As he wandered aimlessly through the cafeteria, beads of sweat dripped down his forehead, stinging his eyes. He felt the copper flecks begin to swirl like a storm. Straining to see through the crowd, he spotted an empty seat at a table in the far corner. The only other occupant was a man with grizzled whiskers who looked like he wanted no part of the camaraderie. Strangely, something about the man's cold exterior drew Stanford toward him. Perhaps he knew instinctively that the man was different from the rest, stronger because he had to be, and that he could provide the sanctuary Stanford desperately sought. It was the strangeness in them both that brought them together. He felt connected to his fellow outcast. Even among the mutants, there were outcasts.

Stanford's legs were heavy as he approached. His heart pounded all the way up to his ears. When he got near, the man looked at him with eyes like shallow, blue pools and said, "You look lost, boy." His voice was deep and growly, not an ember of warmth.

Stanford stared at the man's rough, leathery skin. The creases in his forehead were jagged and carved by years of experience, but there was a paternal quality that brought Stanford comfort. Before he could introduce himself, he heard the man say, "What is wrong with your eyes, boy?"

"I have Wilson's disease," said Stanford. His voice was so weak it sounded as if it came from a faraway place.

The man mulled for a moment. "I've never heard of it. Does it affect your sight?"

"No. I can see fine."

"What causes the dots in your irises?"

"Those are mineral deposits. My body can't expel copper so it stores it in my organs."

"You have copper in your eyes."

Stanford nodded.

The man grunted like it was no big deal. "Is that so? Well, you've come to the right place. Sit down, boy."

Stanford hesitated before taking his place across the table. He watched the man peering curiously over the brim of his coffee mug.

"They call me Iron Man," he said. "We usually sit with our own kind around here, but I'm not one for rule-following. Besides, even though we're not the same, we have some similarities, you and I. You can come to this seat for every break. It will always be here waiting for you."

"What is your disease?" asked Stanford.

"I have too much iron inside. I have to drain my blood from time to time so that my own body doesn't poison me. You don't have to do that, do you?"

Stanford shook his head.

"It's not as bad as it sounds. It actually kept me from being conscripted, so I guess you could say it has its advantages. Not much use for a soldier who has to spill his own blood." The man cracked a half-smile. "What's your name, boy?"

"I'm Stanford."

"Does the copper in your eyes always swirl like that, Stanford?"

"Only when I'm nervous."

"What are you nervous about?"

Stanford shrugged.

"You look awfully young. Were you assigned here by an orphanage?"

"No. I live at home."

"Were your parents conscripted?"

"My parents are dead."

The man looked across the table quietly for a moment. "I'm sorry to hear that. What happened to them? You don't have to tell me if you don't want to. I don't have a lot of tact; an old solitary mutant like me doesn't have time for manners."

"They were in a hover car accident."

"Who takes care of you?"

"I live with an aide, and my dog."

"No siblings?"

Stanford shook his head.

"That's some tough luck, boy, but I'll help you out as much as I can." The man's voice shifted to a more upbeat cadence. "I don't have any family of my own. It will be good for me to help out a young man like you. We can help each other. How does that sound?"

"That sounds good to me."

"It's a deal then, Stanford. What department have you been assigned to?"

"The picking department."

"That's a good place to start. You have nothing to be nervous about. I started in the picking department many years ago. You can learn the business from the ground up. You'll fit in just fine, don't you worry. The first thing we need to do is find you a nickname. All the mutants have them. You don't want to stand out any more than you already do on account of those wild eyes. What's your last name, Stanford?"

"Samuels."

The man sat back and furrowed his brow, accentuating the deep river valleys on his forehead. "Samuels . . . I knew a Stuart Samuels once. He was a sales rep for the eastern sector. I recall he was an Eradicator. Yes, I think that's right. Did you ever hear of a Stuart Samuels?"

Stanford watched a look of recognition draw across the man's weathered features.

"How about that?" laughed the man. "I can't believe I didn't realize it sooner. I can see the resemblance now. You are the Stuart Samuels boy. I remember him saying he had a son with copper in his eyes, but I guess I didn't realize it was so pronounced. It's been a long time since I saw old Stu. I can see him in you, now that I look closely."

Stanford felt his anxiety slowly melting, replaced with a sense of curiosity.

"I got to know your dad from his dealings with the warehouse. He was a good man, Stanford. I'm sorry to hear he's gone. What I can tell you for sure is that he worked incredibly hard to keep your family together."

"I didn't see him much," said Stanford.

"That's due to his job, Stanford. When the war started, he volunteered for reassignment to avoid conscription. He became a special weapons rep, in charge of organizing the distribution of artillery to the front lines. Everything was shipped out of this warehouse. He spent a lot of time here in those days. He had to."

"Did he ever talk about me?"

The man smiled broadly as the memories flashed in his mind. "He spoke about you all the time. His biggest regret was that he had to work so much. What he wanted more than anything was to spend more time with you and your mother. I remember him saying how special you were. Even though he had failed to eradicate the gene, he loved you more than anything in the world. I remember how he used to call you his little king." He paused, searching the cabinets of his mind. "I just assumed your father went on to other things."

Stanford watched the man's blue eyes glaze over. Then, suddenly, he smacked his hand on the table. "I've got it!"

Stanford felt his entire body flinch.

"Your nickname will be Saturn. The copper in your eyes swirls like the rings. It's perfect. What do you think?"

Stanford thought about it. "Okay, Iron Man."

The man expelled a hearty bellow. "It's a pleasure to meet you, Saturn."

The vision of the old man dissipated from Stanford's mind and he found himself back beside the cot in the infirmary tent. He wanted to reach out and take his friend's hand—to return the favor by offering comfort in a time of need. Soon they would share a cup of coffee together and enjoy each other's company, just like old times.

Out the corner of his eye, Stanford saw a flash of movement, followed by the fluttering of the tent flap. He glanced down at his friend one more time before moving quickly toward the exit.

"I have to go, Iron Man."

When he got outside he saw the assassin gesturing for a group of snipers to lower their rifles. "Hold your fire, men! Let the boy go."

Stanford watched the wild child scampering on all fours toward the boundary of the base, churning up a sandstorm in his wake. The child didn't turn back. Within moments he was swallowed by the dark, headed back to his family in the desert.

The assassin instructed the men to return to their posts.

Stanford called to him. "Mr. Dekkar." He trudged across the sand. "You let the boy go."

The assassin nodded. "I knew you wanted it."

"How did you know?"

"I told you before, Mr. Samuels, you talk in your sleep."

Stanford smiled. "Thank you, Mr. Dekkar."

"I trust you, Mr. Samuels. That doesn't mean I always agree with you. But I trust you. How are you feeling?"

"My head has been released from the vice."

"That sounds like progress. Why don't you get some rest and we'll talk later."

"Where are you going?"

"I'm meeting with the inner group. You don't have to concern yourself."

"Can I join you?"

"There's no need. I can relay any pertinent information back to you in the morning."

"I want to come. I'm feeling better."

The assassin nodded. "Okay, Mr. Samuels, let's go."

The assassin led Stanford across the encampment toward the headquarters. Mutants rushed from their residential tents to throw themselves at Stanford's feet, as they always did when he traversed the base. He paused to touch a few supplicants on the head before following the assassin into the main tent.

Inside, a group of soldiers, including Joshua, were huddled around the bank of computers. The monitors showed live aerial images of the Salus dome, quietly glowing from within.

"What have you got for us, men?" asked the assassin.

The soldiers spun around in their chairs to face their superiors. Joshua flinched when he saw Stanford.

The driver of the escort van, Jack, was the first to speak. "The infrareds are detecting a massive heat source from inside the dome."

The assassin sat down in a nearby chair and gestured for Stanford to sit next to him. "What's the source?"

"We're not sure, Mr. Dekkar," said Jack. "The intensity is far stronger than any previous levels detected by the sensors. It's holding strong."

"What are your theories?"

Joshua interjected. "This is off the charts. We know it's not solar. The panels channeling NGC 5866 are not the same energy detected by the thermals."

"How do you know?"

"The levels have spiked overnight. Unless the entire population inside the dome has suddenly turned their thermostats to high, we haven't got a clue what's causing the influx of heat."

The assassin turned to Stanford. "What do you think, Mr. Samuels?"

Stanford glanced at the men. He thought about the dedication it would take to be a member of the Tech Terrorists. All of these men had grown up together, gone to war with one another. This was a way of life. They put their lives on the line every day to fight against the Policy; not because they wanted to, but because they had no choice. They were born into it. He felt small in their presence.

He looked back at the assassin. "I don't have a clue."

"Continue to monitor the levels, men," said the assassin. "Record any fluctuations. If there is a peak, I expect a valley. There must be a logical explanation."

Stanford stared silently at the screen, seeing the outer membrane of the Salus dome pulse like it was breathing. "We have to go back to the transfer compound," he said.

"Why would we go back there?" asked Joshua. "We need to concentrate our efforts on Salus."

"The transfer station is the key to Salus."

"Give it a break, Mr. Samuels," said Joshua. "We've had an aerial drone over the compound since we raided it. The place is vacant. Going back would be a complete waste of time and resources."

The assassin glanced at Stanford. "Why do we need to go back to the compound, Mr. Samuels?"

"Winifred told me the patients would be retrieved."

"And taken where?" asked the assassin.

"To Salus."

Joshua grunted. "Now we're trusting intel from an android? We should have annihilated her with the others. I'm tired of wasting time. Since our appointed leader assumed command, he's done nothing but lead us astray. We need to move forward, but all we do is go backward. I'm not going to stand here and let this charlatan lead us into a deathtrap. Next he'll say we need to go back to the colony again to make sure his dog isn't hungry. Meanwhile, it's a toss-up as to whether our entire camp will freeze to death or suffocate first."

"That's enough, Joshua," said the assassin.

Stanford's eyes ignited, casting Joshua's badly bruised face in a brilliant spotlight.

Joshua glared back. "You can try to intimidate me all you want, Mr. Samuels. I know who you are. You aren't cut out to be a terrorist. You need to relinquish your command."

Stanford felt every muscle in his body tense at once. He considered reaching into his back pocket for the stubby gun, just to put a scare into the man, but he resisted. Instead, he took a step toward the mutant. "My son is inside that dome, Joshua. Never question my desire to get inside Salus again. Do you understand?"

Joshua turned and left the tent without another word.

The assassin placed his hand on Stanford's shoulder. "We'll go back to the transfer station, Mr. Samuels."

Stanford looked at the assassin's damaged face. "We need Winifred."

The assassin smirked. "You're embracing your new leadership role very well. You have passion in you. When you figure out how to channel your power, it will be a beautiful thing."

"How do you know it won't be ugly?"

"I know because the tide has to turn. We've seen too much ugly for too long. It's time for beauty to shine through."

2.26
THE PLAN

The assassin handed the bowl of steaming liquid to Stanford. "You need to drink it while it's hot."

Stanford tipped the concoction down the back of his throat. When he had taken it all in, he passed the bowl back to the assassin and waited for the reaction. "How long will it take?"

"Not long. Lay back and close your eyes."

Stanford rested on the cot and prepared for the sting. "Will you tell me when it's coming?"

"It's better if I don't. Just hold still."

In a moment, Stanford felt a sharp pain in his neck as a microchip was implanted beneath the skin. The sensation reminded him of the injection of I-132. He felt a shiver run along the entire length of his body.

"It's done," said the assassin. "Did it hurt?"

Stanford sat up. "Only a little bit."

"I used a low dose of the fern as an anesthetic. You'll feel numb, but it will wear off in an hour or so." He removed a transponder from his cargo pants. "We'll be able to find you with this."

Stanford rubbed his neck. He could feel the subtle bulge of the implant. "Is it noticeable?"

"It looks like a swollen gland. If they ask, just say you have a sinus infection."

Stanford managed a smile.

The assassin suddenly looked serious. "Stanford, I want you to consider what you are doing. We have trained professionals who can go in your place and execute the mission. I know you don't listen to me, but I wouldn't be doing my job if I didn't tell you that you'd be better off staying here with us. You are valuable to our community. I am asking you to reconsider."

Stanford saw how genuine the man was. He reached across to shake his hand. "Mr. Dekkar, I've spent my whole life laying down. Everything has been stolen from me, and I've done nothing about it. I told your people that I would lead them to Salus. If the path leads directly to failure, then the creator has designs that I just don't understand. Either way, I have to stand up for once."

"You don't need to go on a suicide mission to prove your worth. The greatest leaders are the ones who surround themselves with professionals. Let my men open the dome. We can follow. You will be a god."

"I'm not interested in idolatry. My only concern is finding my son."

"The risk is great, Stanford. I can only send in men who show no visible scars. There are very few."

"It only takes a few to start a revolution. You know that better than anybody."

"I wish I could come with you."

"It's better if you are here."

"I'm sending Joshua. He's the best soldier we have. Do you object?"

Stanford thought a moment. "Do you trust him?"

"I trust him with my life, Mr. Samuels."

"Then I don't object."

"Are you sure I can't talk you out of this?"

Stanford shook his head. "I hope I don't disappoint you."

"You can't disappoint me, Mr. Samuels. From the day I met you in the church, I knew you were the man to lead us. If you can get those Class-5s deactivated, I'll be able to get the rest of my men into Salus."

"When do we leave?"

"The transport is being loaded. We've sedated the patients to induce a prolonged coma."

"Iron Man?"

"He'll stay with us."

Stanford nodded. "Has Winifred been debriefed?"

"Yes, she was resistant at first, but conceded to the plan." The assassin looked at the transponder. "We won't lose you. Shall I give you some time to prepare?"

"No, I'm ready." Stanford slung his legs over the side of the bed and stood up.

Outside the tent, the transport vehicle was being loaded with unconscious solitaries. Several terrorists walked up the ramp to take their place amongst them.

Stanford watched Winifred climb into the cab.

The driver, Jack, leaned out the window of the transport. "Let's go, Mr. Samuels!"

As Stanford walked up the ramp, he locked eyes with the resident mother standing near the community tents. She cradled her surrogate child in her arms, rocking the boy softly in a blanket cocoon. She loved the child as if he were her own.

He saw her mouth the words: *Good luck.*

Supplicants scattered on their knees in the sand as the truck pulled away. Their heads were bowed, hands pressed together in prayer.

Tears streamed down their faces.

Stanford watched them out the rear window until they faded to black. He couldn't help but think that their faith far exceeded his own.

2.27
THE FARMS

A massive Sand Crawler rolled across the dark brown soil of the agricultural section. The flatland had been divided into congruent rectangular plots as far as the eye could see, with multiple solar panels shining energy from the NGC 5866 star upon the fertile ground to encourage germination. Early hints of vegetation had already been coaxed to the surface in perfect garden rows.

The Sand Crawler continued across the soil in the direction of a distant farmhouse. As the vehicle drew near, the sky over the house lit up with brilliant hues of red and orange, followed by a cloud of dense black smoke. Within moments, the entire sky over the agricultural sector was draped in a toxic blanket.

The fields beyond the farmhouse were ablaze with raging columns of flame. Farmhands, dressed in fire retardant gear, scattered for the safety of cement bunkers. The fire ate several hectares of land in an instant. Towering ferns added fuel in the form of pure oxygen released from their fronds, and then collapsed into piles of fertile black ash. Just as quickly as the ferns were consumed, more fronds sprouted up in the mineral-rich soil, growing as tall as the previous plants, only to meet the same fiery death. The cycle continued in perpetual motion.

When the Sand Crawler stopped outside the farmhouse, a Militia man emerged from the vehicle through the side hatch. His head was covered with an insulated hood for protection against the inferno.

A man walked down the front steps of the farmhouse to greet him.

"It feels like we're inside a furnace," said the man.

The Militia man nodded. "How long can it go on for?"

"It's like a forest fire in a forest that has no end. The ferns continue to regenerate. We have to put it out every few hours to allow my men to remove the mounds of ash. We've had a dozen different teams doing shift work on twelve separate fields burning around the clock for the past thirty-six hours."

"How are you not affected by the fumes?"

"Take off your mask and find out for yourself."

The Militia man hesitated.

"Go on," said the farmhand. "Do you see me wearing a mask?"

The Militia man removed his hood and took a deep breath. He felt the clean air rushing through his nostrils.

"Can you feel it opening your lungs?"

"I feel energized."

"That's because it's super-concentrated O2. It floods your blood plasma, giving you a kick of energy. The scientists call it 'mass action'. Can you smell the smoke?"

The Militia man sniffed the air. "No."

"Remarkable, isn't it?"

"How can that be?"

"I don't know. It's like the ferns absorb the impurities."

"It's amazing," said the Militia man. "Why do you think the Patron has ordered the burning?"

The farmhand shrugged. "What the Patron wants, the Patron gets."

The Militia man nodded and looked back toward the truck. "I have another crew."

"Good," said the farmhand. "My men are exhausted. We need help to transport the ash to a field in the northern sector, away from the rest of the crops. We don't want to use up all the arable land in this region. New ferns will grow out of the ash without seeding."

The Militia man shook his head in disbelief.

"Is this the last of them?" asked the farmhand, glancing at the rear gate of the Sand Crawler.

"No. There's one more group to come. I'm headed back to the transfer station right after this."

"Get them here soon. We need all the help we can get."

The Militia man rounded the back of the Sand Crawler and opened the rear hatch. Dozens of men and women were inside, sitting on cots. They appeared disoriented, as if they had just woken from a slumber. The Militia man walked up a ramp into the trailer.

"Welcome to Farmhouse Number Seven. This is your new home," he said. "I know this may seem confusing, but you are perfectly safe as long as you follow orders. Your first direction is to enter the house and find the bunks assigned to you. On the bunks, you will see a fire retardant suit with a number sewn on the breast. You can forget your names; from now on you will be identified by that number. Put on the suit and congregate in the kitchen where you will be fed before we relieve the other shift in the fields. Do you have any questions?"

The solitaries sat still, until finally a man with a cleft lip raised his hand. "Where am I?"

"You are inside Salus," said the Militia man. "Now stand up and exit the vehicle in an orderly fashion. You are a member of the state now."

"I feel sick to my stomach," said the mutant.

"Food will make you feel better. Let's go. Everybody up."

A female solitary spoke. "How did I get here?"

"It doesn't matter how you got here," said the Militia man. "What matters is that you serve the Project. Now stand up."

The solitaries began filing down the ramp, walking toward the farmhouse.

The Militia man turned to the farmhand. "I'll bring you the last batch in less than six hours. Do you have any insubordinates to report?"

"Not yet," said the farmhand. "The drugs seem to have wiped out their memory. They are totally docile, but their output is exemplary."

"The pharmacists can do amazing things with the ferns," said the Militia man.

"What would you do to the subordinates if any were to arise?"

"We'd burn them in the fields with the ferns. See you in six hours."

When the Militia man was back onboard, the Sand Crawler articulated on a pivoting joint and headed back the way it had come.

Overhead, the atmosphere of Salus danced with the fiery hues.

2.28
CAMOUFLAGE

The assassin was huddled around the bank of computers in the main tent with several of his soldiers. The image on-screen was an aerial shot of the transfer station in the desert. The only sign of life was a helix dog that paced the perimeter of the compound before scampering off into the darkness.

"Something spooked the dog," said one of the soldiers.

"Pan left," said the assassin.

The soldier adjusted the control panel to reposition the view of the aerial drone. From the wider angle, the transport vehicle could be seen approaching the front of the compound. When the truck came to a stop, Jack exited the cab, walking around the rear of the trailer to unlatch the hatch. Several physicals jumped out the back and began off-loading the cots. In a few moments, Stanford and Winifred exited from the rear and had a brief conversation with Joshua before heading inside the front door of the compound. Cots bearing unconscious solitaries were ushered into the building.

The assassin stood up from his chair. "Now there's nothing to do but wait."

"How long?" asked one of the soldiers.

"Just keep your eyes on the screens and let me know when something happens."

"Yes, sir."

"Raise the elevation of the drone. I don't want it spotted."

The soldier complied, making another adjustment to raise the camera high above the compound. The lens automatically refocused, but the image was pixilated.

Before the assassin turned to leave, he took one last glance at the screen to watch the grainy image of Joshua following the final cot into the transfer station. When everyone was inside the building, Jack climbed aboard the transport vehicle and started it rumbling across the sand, back in the direction it had come. The compound was silent again, no signs of life.

The assassin reached into his cargo pants to remove the transponder. It showed a set of coordinates that matched the coordinates displayed at the bottom frame on the computer screen.

"I'm going to get some shut-eye," said the assassin. "Call me if anything happens. I don't care how small. Call me even if you see a coyote take a shit in the sand, do you understand?"

"Yes, sir."

He exited the tent, knowing full well there was no way he would sleep a wink.

2.29
PREPARATION

Inside the transfer station, the physicals were busy arranging the cots in rows to match their original locations. Stanford stood to the side, watching on with Winifred.

"Are you okay?" he asked, after a time.

She looked directly at him. "I told you, I'm designed to fight for survival just as much as any human. This mission goes against my programming."

"Then we aren't so dissimilar."

"We are not alike, Mr. Samuels. You are as far from being synthetic as I am from being genuine."

Before Stanford could respond, the EM tubes were ignited above of the cots, illuminating the faces of the solitaries. A voice came from behind.

"Mr. Samuels, you need to get changed."

The voice belonged to Joshua.

Stanford spun around to see Joshua approaching through the aisles. His face was no longer swollen.

"We need to take our positions." Joshua opened his palm to reveal a miniature gun the size of his own thumb. "We won't be able to smuggle our weapons inside, so we're taking these. Don't let the size fool you. It's more than adequate in a fire fight."

Stanford marveled at the tiny weapon.

"There's no trigger. You have to squeeze the handle to fire a round. Apply only minimal force. The safety catch is on the barrel." Joshua set the catch. "The exterior is coated with a dermal adhesive so it'll stick to any part of your skin like a magnet. I suggest you keep it concealed by any means necessary."

"Thank you, Joshua. I'll swallow it if I have to."

"Try not to choke."

Stanford accepted the gun.

"Joshua, whatever happens from here, I want to start fresh. Can we do that?"

"I think we can," said Joshua. "But if this mission fails, and we both make it back alive, I want you to relinquish your duties."

Stanford stared at the soldier for a long moment. He couldn't help but admire the man who fought so hard for what he believed in. He had fought all his life. Even now, with the shadow of Salus bearing down, he battled for every inch.

"That's what this is about?" asked Stanford. "I threaten your status in the hierarchy?"

Joshua grinned. "That's not it, Mr. Samuels. I just don't like you."

"The foster home, where you met Markus . . . it made you who you are."

"I'm a Tech Terrorist, Mr. Samuels. I'll fight until my heart stops beating because it's the only thing I've ever known. Will you relinquish your duties if the mission fails?"

Stanford thought for a moment. "If the mission fails, it won't matter, will it?" He glanced at the android. "Where do I get a hospital gown?"

"Follow me," she said.

The android led Stanford to the surgeons' quarters. Inside were several cots next to a cluster of condensation booths and a changing room. "I will wait for you outside, Mr. Samuels."

Stanford pulled his arms out of his panda jacket and laid it on a cot. "Wait. What are our chances of getting inside?" He began to unbutton his shirt.

"I estimate our chances of getting inside Salus are somewhere between zero-point-five and one percent. Our chances of reaching the PAD are significantly less."

"Seems risky."

The android turned around to give Stanford privacy as he stepped out of his pants.

"I will be disassembled one way or the other," said Winifred. "If I stay here, I will be tortured and then killed. This is the only choice for me, as it is for you."

"You can turn around now."

The android turned to see Stanford in the white hospital gown. He looked like every other mutant patient.

"You're not a soldier, so you must have a verbal shutdown command. Why didn't you ask us to deactivate you?" he asked.

"Would you have spoken the command if I had asked, Mr. Samuels? I may be an artificial intelligence, but I'm not naïve. You need me to get you in."

"You'll be deactivated with the rest of them if we reach the target?"

"The global shutdown extends to all the subseries of Class-5s. I'll be deactivated, but every organism will do what it can to stay alive, even for one more day."

Stanford watched her sit on a cot and begin to remove her shoes. Her previously injured hand was repaired with new flesh.

"I see the ferns heal synthetic tissue."

She glanced at him. "Abandon."

Stanford hesitated. "I'm sorry?"

"Abandon," she repeated. "That's my shutdown command. If I ask you to speak it, you must say it directly to me. Speak clearly, so there is no mistake."

Stanford watched her silently.

"Goodnight, Mr. Samuels."

"Goodnight, Ms. Winifred. Are you going to be okay in here by yourself?"

She glanced back. "I can think of better accommodation. But what choice do I have?"

"I wish it didn't have to be this way."

"What about you, Mr. Samuels? Are you going to be okay lying amongst the solitaries?"

"I can think of better accommodation." Stanford smiled in her direction.

"They say you have no emotional connection to your past, Mr. Samuels, but it seems to me you still do."

"How do you mean?"

The android stood and walked toward the cluster of condensation booths without another word.

2.30
THE HOME

A child of no more than ten years old was seated cross-legged on a bottom bunk in a small, windowless room with bare white walls. Another bunk bed sat empty against the opposing wall, while on the top bunk nearest the door was a child who appeared a few years older than the first, head propped on a pillow. Both children were silent behind open books.

Every once in a while, the younger boy flashed a glance at the elder and then quickly looked back at his book. He was staring at the words more than reading, and when he tried to concentrate, he'd read the same passage over and over until his curiosity forced him to glance back at the boy on the top bunk.

The boy was larger than he was, with broad shoulders and a protruding lump on his throat that signified the onset of puberty. He looked almost like a man, both in appearance and in the confident way he carried himself around the other children. The elder was the first resident he had noticed after his admittance to the home because he stood several inches taller than any of the others; but more than that, it was his imposing personality that made him impossible to ignore. It seemed like no matter where the elder was, his voice was always reverberating down the hallways, finding its way inside every room.

Even now, with both boys quietly turning pages, the elder's mere presence filled the space of the dormitory.

There was a part of the young boy that wanted to be like the elder, to have broad shoulders and walk with the same kind of swagger, but there was another piece of him that wondered what was missing in the boy that he compensated for with intimidation tactics.

He looked back at his book, staring at the words without reading.

The peace was broken when a robot aide stuck its head inside the room. "Wash up and report for dinner, boys."

The older boy responded with a deep, mature voice. "We're trying to enrich our lives with good literature. Can you close the door?"

The aide disappeared, clicking the latch.

The elder looked toward his junior. "Don't think I haven't noticed you watching me. Do you have something to say?"

The young child shook his head.

"Are you sure? You've seemed awfully curious about me ever since you arrived. Or maybe you just act weird when you're uncomfortable. This place is hard to get used to, but you'll settle in. The routines will become second nature after a while. Do you have any questions about the place so far?"

The boy was silent, even though he could tell the elder was reaching out.

The older boy dangled his legs over the side of the bunk. "You've been here two days, and I haven't heard you talk yet. Are you one of those mutes?"

The boy shook his head.

"Well if you aren't mute, why won't you talk? You're going to have to say something sooner or later. Why don't you tell me about the book you're reading?"

The youngster desperately wanted to speak, but the words would not come.

The elder jumped off the top bunk, snatching the book from the child's hands and investigating the cover. "This is a fairy tale," he said. "It's not even real."

The youngster stared back with wide eyes.

"Say something," said the older boy. "Say something or I'll hit you." He cocked his arm back. "If you don't tell me your name right now, I'm going to break your nose."

Tears welled in the young child's eyes. His natural response was to flinch, but he knew he needed to project an image of strength, no matter what the consequence. His survival instinct told him that if he didn't stand up to the bigger boy now, he'd never gain his respect. From out his lips escaped a single word. "Markus." He tried to keep his chin from quivering.

"What's that? Speak up."

"My name is Markus." His voice was firmer now as he did his best to put on a brave face.

"You have a voice after all. How do you do, Markus? My name is Clint."

The older boy reached out to shake.

Markus' hand felt small and weak by comparison.

"Was that so hard? There's no need to be scared. I provide all my roommates with protection. You are the last person who should be scared. All the rest of them, that's who should be worried." He tossed the book over his shoulder.

"You don't want to be reading that fake crap anymore. You need a reality check. I have some reading material that will interest you. It's just for the people in this room. We're the inner circle."

Clint lifted his mattress and pulled out a stack of loose pages hidden beneath. "My uncle wrote this. He has a way with words." He handed the pages to Markus. "It's a story about a terrorist cell under the ground. They live in caves. They are against the Policy. This isn't fantasy. This is real stuff. It will make you smarter. Do you know how I know that?"

"How?"

"I know because I'm older. Older people know more than younger people. It's just how it is. My uncle told me that. He knows just about everything."

The boy stared at the document without reading it.

"You're one of us now, Markus. I see how you watch people, observing them. You're quiet but you're always thinking. You would make a good silent assassin." Clint ripped the pages from the child's hands and put them back under the mattress. "If you tell anybody about what I just showed you, I'll cut your head off while you sleep, do you understand?"

The boy nodded. He felt his stomach churning like he was about to vomit.

"Let's go for dinner."

When the boys reached the cafeteria, they found their assigned seats next to the other four boys who shared their bunk room.

"What kind of slop are we having today?" asked Clint.

The other boys remained silent.

A robot aide approached the table with a tray of food.

Clint leaned over to smell the offering. "This is wretched," he said. "It looks like a mound of albino shit."

The aide peered back with electronic eyes. "Would you like me to remove your plate?"

Clint sneered. "No. Go away. Albino shit is my favorite."

The aide returned to the kitchen.

As soon as the robot was gone, Clint looked around at the boys and leaned in to speak quietly. "My uncle says life is what we make of it. We aren't defined by what a bunch of robots tell us to do. We need to maintain our individual selves. Are you with me?"

The boys glanced at each other and shrugged, not sure what he was talking about.

Clint peered at Markus. "Watch this," he said with a sly grin. "I'll show you what kind of idiots we're dealing with."

He climbed on the tabletop with his dish of slop to address the cafeteria. "Excuse me, can I get your attention? I don't mean to interrupt your gourmet dinner, but I just wanted to know, with a show of hands, how many of you realize you are eating albino shit?"

Just like that, every mutant in the cafeteria paused to look at the young man standing on the table.

"I know this may sound disgusting, but I have a refined palate, and I know albino shit when I'm eating it. There is a certain distinct aroma and texture that is unmistakable." Clint took a big spoon of the slop and put it in his mouth before spitting it back on the plate with a look of utter repulsion. "Yep, that's albino shit all right!"

A single voice called out. "Don't cause trouble. Just eat your food."

Clint scanned the crowd for the source of the voice. "Who has the guts to talk back to me?"

A pale-faced boy with light-colored hair stood up from a table. "I do."

Clint burst into exaggerated laughter. "An albino! Thank you for providing your excrement for our meals! We all owe you a big round of applause. Let's hear it for the albino, everybody!"

The cafeteria was suddenly alive with a chorus of applause and awkward laughter.

"Get off the table," shouted the albino. His fists were clenched so tightly that his arms vibrated with tension. "What makes you think you're better than everybody else?"

"It's because I'm older," said Clint. "And you better watch your mouth if you know what's good for you."

"I bet your parents weren't even conscripted," said the albino. "They probably dropped you off here because they couldn't stand you anymore. Their lives are better off without you."

Clint's face went immediately dark.

A hush fell over the cafeteria.

The albino held his gaze before retaking his seat.

Clint was perfectly still for a moment before throwing his plate of slop in the direction of the albino. It shattered on the floor and splattered on unintended targets. In a matter of seconds, several robot aides surrounded Clint's table and reached to get the boy down.

Clint avoided their grasps, kicking wildly at their metallic arms.

"Get down at once," demanded an aide.

The young man leaped off the table, managing to elude their clutches, and charged at the albino boy. The residents sitting at the same table as the albino stood up to defend their roommate. At once, the entire cafeteria was in disorder. Boys from every table stood up to engage in a fight they had not started.

Markus closed his eyes and felt his chest heaving. He tried desperately to hold off the tears. All he wanted was to return to his room and bury his head under the covers.

He felt a reassuring hand on his shoulder.

"Let's get out of here," said a voice.

Markus followed the voice back to his room. When he sat down on his bunk, he looked across at the familiar face of one of his roommates.

Sounds of commotion continued to reverberate through the walls.

"Are you okay?" asked the boy.

Markus nodded. "Yes."

The other child smiled. "I didn't know you could speak. What's your name?"

"My name is Markus, what's yours?"

"I'm Joshua."

Joshua flopped on the bottom bunk below Clint's bed. There was a childish quality about his appearance. His cheeks were round and pudgy, his neck absent of a bulging Adam's apple.

Markus felt comfortable in his presence.

"It will get better, Markus. You just have to train your mind to stop caring. Once you do that, nothing else matters."

"Is that what you did?"

194

"More or less," said Joshua. "It takes time to master."

"How long have you been here?"

"Not long. Just a few weeks, but I'm trying to get out."

"How?"

"I don't know yet. Clint says his uncle can provide safe passage for anybody who agrees to join his group, but I don't know how much of what Clint says is true. He's kind of a jerk, but I'm keeping him close just in case. You're a part of his inner circle now so you might as well keep him close too."

"What if I don't want to be in his circle?"

"You don't have a choice. Just agree with everything he says. That's what I do. And don't tell anybody about those papers under his mattress. He's real touchy about that."

"He said he'd cut off my head if I told anybody."

Joshua burst into laughter. "He did?"

Markus nodded.

"He's a jerk, Markus, but I don't think he'd cut off your head. I think you'll be okay. He just talks tough."

The boys sat in silence for a moment.

Joshua put his head down on the pillow. "What happened to your parents?"

"What do you think?"

"We have to stick together, okay, Markus?"

"Okay."

"We can't let them break us. That's one thing Clint said that I agree with. We have to maintain our loyalty to one another. We aren't defined by this place."

The door burst open. Two robot aides entered carrying Clint's limp, unconscious body, depositing him on the top bunk. Blood leaked from the elder's nose.

"Lights out early tonight," said one of the aides.

The room went dark as the door latched.

"Goodnight, Markus," said Joshua.

"Goodnight, Joshua," said Markus.

The sounds of Clint's labored breathing filled the darkness. Even unconscious, his presence was all encompassing.

2.31
CAPTURE

"Mr. Dekkar, wake up!"

The assassin shot upright. He appeared disoriented as his eyes focused on the figure of the soldier standing near the flap of the tent.

"What is it?"

"The Militia has arrived at the transfer station."

The assassin threw his legs over the side of the cot.

When he arrived at headquarters, he rushed toward the bank of computer monitors. "Tell me what's happening." His body surged with adrenaline.

The grainy image on-screen showed a Sand Crawler out front of the compound. Several Militia men had exited the vehicle and were walking to the entrance of the building. A ramp at the rear of the truck was extended on the sand.

"When did they arrive?" asked the assassin.

"Not more than two minutes ago, sir."

"Lower the elevation of the probe by ten feet."

The soldier at the control panel adjusted the height of the drone. The image became moderately sharper.

Several minutes went by without incident until a helix dog came on-screen, wandering in from the surrounding desert. It sat down by the Sand Crawler, wagging its tail as it waited for the men to come out of the building.

The assassin groaned. "How many of those damn dogs are there?" He began pacing the tent.

Within moments, the first cot appeared out the front of the compound, carried by a Militia man on either side.

"Sir, they're back."

The assassin watched the Militia load the cot into the back of the Sand Crawler. A second cot appeared soon after, followed by a third. Soon a steady stream of cots was escorted out of the transfer station and loaded into the back of the massive vehicle.

The assassin strained to identify the patients. "I can't see their faces. Can you lower the elevation?"

"Are you sure, sir?"

"Yes, I'm sure. Drop it another ten feet."

The soldier lowered the drone, allowing the lens to zoom in on the cots from a closer vantage. Now the faces of the patients were clearly visible.

The assassin stared intently at the images of the unconscious solitaries as they were escorted into the vehicle. Amongst the patients was the face of Joshua. He was as still as if he was dead. The assassin watched his friend taken up the ramp into the back of the Sand Crawler.

At the corner of the screen, the helix dog wandered toward a cot that had just left the building. The dog began to circle the Militia men, sniffing and barking.

"What the hell is that dog doing?" asked the assassin. "Change the angle. Zoom in."

The camera rotated to get a better look. When it zoomed in, it captured Stanford's face on the monitor. His eyes were closed, his body appearing like just another coma-tose patient.

The Militia men attempted to shoo the dog away but it kept coming back. At one point, it reared up and put its front paws on the side of the cot, nearly tipping it over.

The assassin yelled at the screen. "Goddamn it! Get the hell away, dog. Get lost!"

The dog circled around again, determined to alert the men about the intruder, but got tangled in one of the Militia men's feet. The Militia man gave the dog a swift kick and sent it scurrying away. Stanford's supine body was ushered into the vehicle with the others.

The assassin sat down in front of the monitor and wiped his sweaty brow. He felt his heart pounding inside his chest like it was going to burst forth. When he looked back at the monitor, he saw the android, Winifred, walking slowly beside a Militia man. She was involved in an extended conversation.

"Key on the android," said the assassin.

The camera zoomed in on the woman.

She walked alongside the Militia man for a few more feet before peeling off and climbing aboard the cab of the Sand Crawler.

The assassin exhaled deeply and rubbed his temples. "I hope we can trust her," he said.

"What if they find the other Class-5s, sir?" asked one of the soldiers.

"Mr. Samuels assured me that the android would take care of it."

"What's she going to tell them?"

"She's going to bend the truth. She'll say that the base was raided but she avoided detection."

On screen, the helix dog scampered into the Sand Crawler. When the ramp retracted, all the doors were secured and the vehicle's engine stirred up a dense cloud of dust before driving out of frame into the lonely desert.

"Do you want me to follow with the drone?" asked the soldier at the controls.

"No," said the assassin. "The anti-tracking device will throw us off anyway. Abandon it."

"Are you sure?"

"Stop asking me if I'm sure and just do it."

As soon as the Sand Crawler was out of range, the transmission on the computer monitor faded to black.

"What now, sir?"

"Load the trucks," said the assassin.

"How many?"

"All of them."

The assassin walked across the encampment toward the residential tents. The desert seemed quieter than usual. Even the supplicants were staying inside tonight. When he reached his tent he flopped down on the bunk and removed the transponder from his cargo pants. The coordinates showed steady progress toward Salus.

Good luck, Mr. Samuels. Good luck.

2.32
THE DOME

For miles, the only sound inside the Sand Crawler was the almost imperceptible churning of treads across the barren landscape. The interior of the trailer was as black as the moonless sky.

Stanford resisted the urge to open his eyes, even to take a quick glance around. Despite his best efforts to remain calm, he didn't have faith that he could control his eyes under the circumstances. He couldn't risk illuminating the entire trailer and alerting the Militia.

Instead, he drifted off into his own mind, picturing the dense forest of ferns near the Salus dome. He wandered through the tall stalks, looking for the clearing where the wild children had sat around the shallow pool. The forest was thick, and he struggled to find his way. He walked for several minutes before stopping to take a break. From somewhere behind he heard a female voice.

"Stanford, this way."

"Who's there?"

There was no response. He followed the origin of the voice, pushing past the tall stalks while trying to keep his footing. It didn't take long before he had lost his way.

"Where are you?" he called.

"Stanford, I'm over here," said the voice.

"I can't see you."

Stanford could hear footfalls moving toward him. Soon, the naked figure of Winifred appeared through the fronds, her face and neck bearing the marks of fresh scar tissue.

"Do you see me now?" she asked.

"Yes. You've been hurt."

"Come with me."

"Where are we going?"

"I'm taking you to Salus."

He followed the android through the brush, trying to stay as close as possible. When they reached a small clearing, she turned around to expose her bare torso. Her dark hair teased him, obscuring the contours of her perfectly formed breasts.

"What are you doing?"

"I have never experienced love, Mr. Samuels. Will you make me feel it?"

Stanford stared at her nudity. "You said you would take me to Salus."

"This is something you need to do for me in exchange."

"This isn't love," he said.

"I've seen how you look at me. I want to feel you inside me." The woman approached, wrapping her arms around his neck. "Do this for me and I'll give you what you want."

Stanford was on top of her on the forest floor, pushing into her with a soft, gentle rhythm. It was effortless to mount her, like he had done it before.

"Love me harder, Mr. Samuels. I want to feel it!"

Stanford pushed with more intensity. Beads of sweat gathered on his forehead.

All around, the ferns ignited in a sea of ferocious flames, screeching in agony as they were burned. The fire spread

202

quickly, leaping from frond to frond, creating a thick cloud of smoke that covered their naked bodies over like a blanket.

Stanford felt the android's nails piercing his back. His skin began to perspire; the smoke stung his eyes. Through bleary vision he traced his eyes along the raised scars on the side of her face, from the top of her cheek all the way down her neck to the blades of her shoulders.

"Love me, Mr. Samuels. Love me!"

"Who hurt you, Winifred?"

The woman moaned with pleasure as her pupils constricted. "Don't you recognize me, Stanford? I am Ilsa K." She gripped him with enough force to compress his lungs. "I escaped the helix dogs. How could you have forgotten me?"

Stanford could not speak. He pressed his eyelids together and listened to the ferns screaming like stuck pigs as they were consumed and turned to ash.

Everything went black . . .

"This is Transport Unit 345, requesting permission to enter Salus."

The voice brought Stanford back from his dream.

He felt the vehicle begin to slow beneath him.

A different voice crackled over the radio. "Vehicle 345, please state your purpose."

"Requesting delivery of post-op mutant cargo," said the first voice.

There was a short delay.

"Permission granted, Unit 345. Proceed to the inspection station."

The vehicle accelerated, and Stanford immediately felt a fluttering in his chest. He clenched his fists together, trying to repress the adrenaline coursing through his veins. He couldn't help but recall the time he had breached the wall of the Perfect colony. It had been so built up in his mind that he could only fantasize about it in his dreams; and when it finally happened after nearly a lifetime of anticipation, he felt nothing at all. There was no euphoria, no feelings of exultation. The experience had left him numb.

Now, passing into Salus, he felt an entirely different sensation. The emotions swelling through his body were intense and real. He envisioned himself jumping up from the cot and opening the trailer door to glimpse the outside world. He wanted to view utopia with his own eyes. What would it look like? Would it resemble the forest and the babbling brook depicted on the ceiling in the lobby of the Central Tower? What was the picture of paradise? He could only imagine.

Sounds of traffic suddenly attacked his ears. His vision of the forest was replaced by a concrete landscape. He saw skyscrapers in his mind, tall and intimidating, with fiery explosions dancing in the sky. He was flooded by images of superhighways splitting into circuitous interchanges leading to a metropolis of buildings so tall they touched the top of the dome. The urban sector was a beating heart—the roads were the capillaries feeding the various artificial environments.

The conflicting images confused him. He needed to regain control.

Don't leave me, God. If you only grant me one thing in this life, please let me find my son.

The truck came to a stop, and he could hear the trailer door opening.

"We're here."

The voice belonged to Winifred.

Another voice spoke: "Point out the insurgents."

Footsteps were suddenly inside the trailer, walking between the cots.

"This is one," said Winifred.

Stanford heard the sounds of struggle. He kept his eyelids firmly clenched.

"And this is another," said Winifred.

Joshua's voice bellowed through the darkness. "Get your hands off me!"

Stanford couldn't bear it any longer. He opened his eyes and saw Winifred standing over him.

"And this is another," she said, pointing her finger in his face.

Two strong arms grabbed Stanford by the shoulders and dragged him off the cot. The arms forced him to the edge of the trailer and tossed his body off the back. He landed in a heap next to the other Tech Terrorists on the floor of a large warehouse. Dozens of Class-5 soldiers surrounded them, weapons drawn.

Joshua reached inside his gown for his gun, but a Class-5 approached and knocked him across the head.

Winifred addressed Stanford. "Tell your men to drop their weapons, Mr. Samuels."

Stanford looked about his group.

Nothing needed to be said. The men dropped their guns on the cement floor and were immediately bound in shackles.

"They promised not to disassemble me," said Winifred, staring into Stanford's wild eyes. "It was a last minute deal."

A soldier patted Stanford down before binding his hands.

"Conduct a thorough body cavity search on Mr. Samuels," said Winifred. "His weapon is well concealed."

Stanford glared at the android. "This was your plan all along."

"I told you your obsession would be the end of you," said Winifred. "Salus was a delusion. I have to commend you for your effort, but it ends here. I have ensured that you won't be tortured like your men did to me, but the same can't be said for the rest of them."

"I should have murdered you when I had the chance," spat Joshua.

Winifred addressed one of the Class-5s. "Put that man in the dog cage first. Make sure he suffers."

The soldiers began dragging the terrorists across the floor toward a rear door.

"Let me go," screamed Joshua. "Don't touch me!"

One of the last to be restrained was Winifred.

"What are you doing?" she said, trying to pull away. "We made a deal. You promised I would be spared."

"We promised you'd be spare parts," said the Class-5.

"You can't do this," she shrieked. "I fulfilled my obligation. I delivered the Tech Terrorists!"

Another Class-5 approached the front of the Sand Crawler to address the driver. "Take your remaining cargo to Farmhouse Seven."

As soon as the vehicle's engine rumbled to life, the bay door opened, introducing processed sunlight from the outside world.

Beyond the garage was Salus, an environment that presently seemed about as far from utopia as possible.

As the Sand Crawler exited and the bay door closed, there was only darkness and the shrieks of captive men.

2.33
ACCIDENT

Stanford stared out the living room window as his father fed the well-manicured lawn with a water hose. Despite the twin suns beating down at midday, his father wore formal pants and a button-down shirt with long sleeves. Stanford couldn't help but notice his father's pale complexion.

His mother called out from the kitchen. "Stanford, honey, I made you a sandwich for dinner, and if you get hungry later, there are snacks in the pantry."

"Why didn't you just let the babysitter do that, Mom?"

She arrived at his side, kissing him on the cheek. "I like doing things for my son."

Stanford watched his mother make her way toward the door. She looked radiant in a navy blue sleeveless dress and black heels.

"You look nice, Mom."

She smiled. "Thank you, honey. It seems like forever since your father and I met at the coupling ball. As a matter of fact, that may be the last time I can even remember going out for dinner and dancing."

A robot aide entered from the kitchen. "You look positively splendid, Mrs. Samuels. Happy Anniversary."

Stanford's mother chuckled. "You are very sweet, thank

you." She looked at her son. "One day I hope to be invited to your coupling ball, Stanford."

Stanford rolled his eyes.

"We shouldn't be too late. Call us if there's an emergency. We have the portables."

"Stanford is in good hands," said the aide. "As per colonial regulations, I have all seven levels of first aid. There is no situation I have not successfully dealt with in the past. You need not worry."

"I have all confidence in you, as does Mr. Samuels. Thank you."

"You are welcome, Mrs. Samuels."

Stanford's mother flashed a smile at her son. "I'll check on you when I get home."

"Bye, Mom. Have fun."

He watched through the window as she walked down the path to the hover car. His father turned off the hose and dried his hands on his pants before approaching the driver's seat. The car lifted off the road and accelerated out of his vision.

When they were gone, he turned back to the robot aide. "Let's get some food."

The aide turned to follow, watching as Stanford rifled through the pantry.

"Your mother made you a wonderful sandwich, Stanford."

"I don't want a sandwich." He found a bag of salty junk food and ripped it open like a savage.

"Your mother would not want you to ingest empty calories for dinner, Stanford. It is completely void of all essential nutrients. Your blood sugar levels will drop and your insulin levels will spike, putting undue stress on your metabolism."

"Do you always talk like that?"

"I don't compute."

"I'll eat what I want to eat. And if you tell my mother, I'll make sure you don't babysit for me again."

"It is unethical for me to turn a blind eye to irresponsible behavior."

Stanford took a mouthful of the junk food. "You talk too much."

"What about the sandwich, Stanford? What will your mother say when she notices you didn't touch it?"

"You eat it."

"I am a robot aide. I was not designed with a digestive system."

"So throw it down the garbage disposal. You are highly qualified. Figure it out for yourself."

Stanford took his bag of junk food into the living room and flopped down on the couch in front of the video screen. Out the window, he saw the twin suns were low on the horizon.

He pressed the button on the remote and flipped absently through the channels. Sounds and pictures flashed on the screen, but he couldn't focus on anything for more than a few minutes.

The old boy jumped up on the couch and snuggled next to him.

"You're not supposed to be on the couch, old boy. You're only up here because you know Mom isn't here to swat you."

The dog settled his head on Stanford's lap, with not a care in the world.

"Sleep well, old boy. Sleep well."

The robot aide entered the living room, looking rather flustered. "Stanford, I have been told in no uncertain terms that the dog is not allowed on the couch."

Stanford looked back with his mouth full. "If you worry too much you can get high blood pressure, which leads to heart attack and stroke."

"I don't have a heart or a brain," said the aide. "I am entirely electronic."

Stanford laughed, spraying bits of food particles onto the living room floor.

"Oh dear, now look at the mess you've made." The aide quickly went to fetch a Quic-Vac device.

Stanford turned his attention to the video screen. The image showed a procession of young children being led by robot aides into a building. The sign over the front door read: *Orphanage of Lost Souls.*

Stanford turned up the volume to hear the voice of the newscaster.

"This is a scene that is becoming more frequent with each passing week. As the war with the Tech Terrorists continues to wage, more and more families on either side of the walls are being split apart to fulfill their patriotic duty. These are the children left behind—filing into orphanages just like this one each and every day. And as the enemy line draws closer to the civilized sector, the number of lost souls will continue to mount."

The robot aide returned to the living room with the vacuum device, quickly sucking up the mess on the floor. "I would appreciate a modicum of respect, Stanford. My duty as a babysitter is to provide the best care possible, and in order to fulfill my obligation, I require a certain amount of mutual buy-in. I can't have you purposely trying to sabotage this arrangement for your own personal amusement."

Stanford watched the video screen in solemn silence.

The aide turned his head toward the broadcast. "Stanford, what are you watching?"

Stanford looked back at the robot aide. His mischievous nature had vanished. "Will I be taken to an orphanage?"

"Why would you be taken to an orphanage? You are perfectly cared for at home."

"But what if my parents are conscripted?"

"That is impossible. Your father has ensured that you will stay here, in this house, for as long as you choose. There is no need to worry."

"But what happens if they die?"

"Stanford, your parents are not going to die. Even in the unlikely event of the most tragic accident imaginable, which I calculate to be somewhere between the odds of one and one-point-six percent, you have been provided for. Your father has invested in a trust fund that affords you a robot aide from the Ministry of Youth and Families for as long as you require support. You will never be sent to an orphanage."

"What will happen to those boys?"

"What boys, Stanford?"

"The boys in the orphanage."

"They will be cared for until they can be returned to their families, I imagine."

"What happens if their parents don't come back?"

"It is not for me to say what will happen, Stanford. My only duty is to care for you. Now turn off the video screen before you give yourself nightmares."

Stanford pressed the button on the remote. The screen went black. He felt the dog twitching beside him.

"Do you promise I will never go to one of those places?"

"I promise," said the aide. "Now let's go dispose of that sandwich and arrange the pantry so Mrs. Samuels doesn't notice the missing bag of junk food."

Stanford smiled and got up from the couch. "Okay." He patted the robot aide on the shoulder like an old friend.

2.34
THE TOUR

When Stanford's eyes snapped open he saw the ceiling of the jail cell. Next to his cot was nothing more than a toilet bowl between four cement walls. He felt an urgent churning in his stomach. He got up quickly and stumbled toward the toilet, vomiting into the dirty bowl. Wiping the stomach acid from his mouth, he saw a well-dressed man in a white tailored suit standing at the entrance to his cell.

Stanford's voice was weak. "Are you enjoying the view?"

The man smirked.

"Am I dead?"

"If you're dead, then I don't know what that makes me." The man entered the cell and dropped articles of clothing on Stanford's cot.

"What are those?"

"I'm going to take you out of here."

"Why?" Stanford spit into the bowl.

"I'll tell you everything in time, but for now, you need to get dressed."

"What if I want to stay?"

The man looked around the cell. "That's up to you. You have one minute to make up your mind. I'll be waiting in the hall."

Stanford watched the man exit the cell. When he was alone again he forced his body to sit upright. There was no reason to stay. Whatever was in store for him, it was better to get it over with now.

He got off the cold floor and changed into the freshly laundered shirt and overalls that had been delivered by the mysterious man. His eyes began to glow as he followed the man down the hallway.

"Your eyes are unique," said the man, "but I also know they have caused you grief. I know the depth of suffering you have experienced. It's why I want to take you out."

"How do you know about me?"

The man smiled. "We can't talk here. The walls have ears. Follow my lead and everything will be okay."

More prison cells lined the hallway on either side. In every filthy cell, Stanford saw comatose prisoners lying on cots without sheets. He couldn't bear to look at the squalid conditions.

"They are androids, Mr. Samuels; old generation robots that are no longer able to carry out their programming. This is where they are held."

"Held for what?"

"I'm glad you asked that." When they reached the end of the hall, the mysterious man unlocked a steel door. "Can you dim those rays, Stanford? We want to be as inconspicuous as possible."

Stanford took a moment to calm his body until the beams disappeared from his eyes.

On the other side of the door was a room the size of an airport hangar. The floor was stacked with massive bins loaded with severed appendages and other robot parts. Two men in blue overalls crossed their path, holding a transparent sack stuffed with a woman's severed head.

Stanford overheard one man say to the other: "I guess the nurturing department is in line for a new head nurse."

The other man grinned. "If she still had a head, I bet she'd think twice about releasing the wild children who were earmarked for the farms."

Stanford turned to watch the men as they passed by. He heard his guide speak.

"This is the disassembly station. The mechanics call it the chop shop. It's where parts are salvaged from older androids and repurposed in newer models. A lot of the superficial parts, like torsos and heads and appendages, can be installed without any loss of functionality. It saves on manufacturing costs."

"Why did you bring me here?"

"You are an inquisitive man, Stanford. I like that about you. Come with me."

They continued across the cement floor toward a jail cell. As they got near, Stanford could see Winifred behind the bars, sitting on the floor in the center. A mechanic in blue overalls stood outside the cell, oiling the teeth of a chainsaw.

Stanford locked eyes with Winifred.

The mechanic looked up from the blade. "What can I do for you, gentlemen?"

"I'm from the PAD," said the well-dressed man, flashing an identification badge from his breast pocket. "And this is Stanford Samuels. He presently works in the shipping division but aspires to be a mechanic. I offered to show him what you do. I hope you don't mind."

"I don't mind at all," said the mechanic. "If you had come one minute later, you would have missed the show."

"I'm glad we arrived when we did," said the well-dressed man.

The mechanic picked up the chainsaw and stepped inside the jail cell. "This is the time I would normally say the keyword command to deactivate the robot before the dismemberment. It's sort of like having mercy on them. They don't like pain, but this android won't be deactivated."

"Why is that?" asked the well-dressed man.

"Orders from the Patron. I just follow the directive."

"I understand," said the well-dressed man. "This actually works out quite well. Stanford will be able to get an understanding of everything the job entails."

The android's features twisted in horrific anticipation. She pleaded through the bars. "Please, Mr. Samuels, speak the command."

The mechanic glanced at Stanford. "You two know each other?"

"Mr. Samuels has no connection to the unit," said the well-dressed man. "She overheard our introductions and this is her desperate plea to save herself. Stanford is here only as an observer. He has no authority to speak the command."

Stanford watched tears leak out Winifred's eyes. He resisted stepping toward her only because he knew it wouldn't make any difference. He had rescued her from a cage once, but this time he was powerless. He closed his eyes—he couldn't bear to witness torture. For as much as she had done to harm the mission, he would not watch her final moments. She had sealed her own fate. She had predicted her end.

"Please proceed," said the well-dressed man.

216

"All right." The mechanic fired up the chainsaw and put his protective goggles in place.

Winifred clutched the bars. "Please spare me. I beg of you."

Her words were drowned out by the sound of the saw.

With a single motion, the blade severed Winifred's head from her torso. Her body crumpled to the ground; the head settled in the middle of the jail cell, leaking fluid.

Stanford felt a violent churning in his stomach as he opened his eyes. He breathed deeply in an effort to keep his irises calm.

"Are you feeling okay, Mr. Samuels?" The well-dressed man dabbed his suit with a tissue to soak up stray spots of black fluid.

The mechanic removed his goggles and set down the chainsaw. "I'm sorry. I should have warned you about the spray."

"No problem. Thank you for allowing us to watch you in action. You've been very helpful. It's time to go, Mr. Samuels. There is a car waiting to take you back to the shipping division."

Stanford took one last glance at Winifred's decapitated head—an expression of horror frozen on her face—before following the man across the hangar toward the exit.

A hover car waited on the street.

"I hope you appreciate what you just saw, Mr. Samuels."

"Why did you show me that?"

"I know how she betrayed you. Salus is a better place without her."

"How do you know she betrayed me?"

The man grinned. "Get in the car, Stanford. There's so much more."

"Who are you?"

"I'm someone who wants to help you."

"What about the others? What have you done to them?"

"This isn't about the others. This is about you."

The side hatches opened and both men slid into the back seats.

"Forgive me, Mr. Samuels, but I'm going to have to bind your hands. It's only while we travel in the car."

A pair of metal shackles ejected from the rear console. Stanford secured his wrists in the restraints.

"Thank you for understanding." The man leaned forward to tap the driver on the shoulder. "Let's go," he said.

The vehicle lifted off the ground and proceeded through the urban sector. Stanford watched the tall buildings streak across the windows and couldn't help but think of the Perfect colony. The downtown core was familiar to him. It was as if he had walked the streets of Salus before.

"Look ahead," said the well-dressed man.

Through the windshield was a perfect replica of the Personal Associations Division. The massive Central Tower was sandwiched by two squatty buildings, the entire compound surrounded by iron gates.

"It was copied down to the finest detail, Mr. Samuels. Every nook and cranny of the original PAD has been duplicated inside Salus. I can tell by your expression that you are impressed."

Stanford felt a swell of emotion as he caught sight of a street sign that announced Idyllic Avenue. He craned his neck to stare up at the Central Tower, all the way to the seventeenth floor.

"It's a remarkable place, isn't it? The city planners

outdid themselves. The entire urban sector is a testament to their hard work."

Stanford turned to watch the building fade through the rear window as the hover car left the downtown core.

The well-dressed man pressed a button on the console, raising a tinted glass partition between the driver and the rear seats.

"We can speak in confidence now, Mr. Samuels. The driver can no longer hear us. I know your boy was in that building. I know you are suffering."

Stanford looked into the man's dark eyes. "How do you know so much about me?"

"There's so much I have to show you. Watch closely and you'll find the answers."

Stanford felt the pain return to his stomach.

The man gestured out the side window. "Look there."

Outside, Stanford could see rolling, grassy plains. A jackrabbit scampered into a patch of woods to escape a hungry coyote.

In the distance, a herd of buffalo grazed on the short grass.

"This is utopia, Stanford. Look at it. Every environment you can imagine is here to enjoy. Mankind won. We conquered Ultim."

The vehicle crossed into the savanna, passing by a pride of lions sunning themselves under an acacia tree. Out the other window, a pod of hippopotami bathed in a muddy river.

"Have you ever hunted an elephant, Stanford?"

"No."

"Let's go big game hunting." The man lowered the partition to signal the driver to stop.

"I'll wait for you here, sir," said the driver as the vehicle lowered to the ground.

The well-dressed man removed Stanford's shackles and popped the side hatch. "Come get a rifle, Stanford."

Stanford followed around to the rear as the trunk popped automatically. Inside were two hunting rifles.

"I always keep two handy, just in case an opportunity such as this arises."

The man selected one and handed the other to Stanford.

They waded through the tall grass until they came upon a marsh. Several black-headed herons wandered the banks in search of food.

The well-dressed man crouched in the grass and gestured for Stanford to do the same.

"I'm glad I can share this with you, Stanford."

"Why?"

"I admire you. I have been watching you since you were a child. You have struggled with a miraculous disease your whole life; you have faced unimaginable odds, yet here you are. You are incredibly strong. You are the type of person I want to be associated with. I'd like you to join my ranks."

"What are you talking about?"

"There's an open position that I would like you to consider. You'd be working directly beneath me, managing my entire organization. You may not have the experience of the other candidates, but you have the intangible qualities that are much more important. Mr. Samuels, I'd like you to be the new Executive Director of the Personal Associations Division."

Stanford glanced at the man in silence, and for first time, he knew the beady, dark eyes staring back belonged to the Patron.

"It's a lot to take in, I realize. You don't have to decide this very instant. Mull it over."

"You look different on the video screens," said Stanford.

The man grinned. "It's a persona, Stanford. The image is a fabrication. My identity has always been protected, even altered when necessary, for obvious reasons. The PAD has taken good care of me over the years, making sure I get my regular tune-ups. When you are in a position of authority, there will always be people who want to stab you in the back, even in your own ranks. You will have to get used to that. The fact that I'm revealing myself is indicative of my trust in you." He pointed forward through the tall grass.

An elephant was wading into the marsh to cool off.

"I want you to join me, Mr. Samuels."

"What about my son?"

"Your son is safe."

"Where is he?"

"I'll take you to him. But first we need to get ourselves an elephant."

The majestic beast collected water with its trunk and doused its hot, leathery skin.

"This is your shot, Mr. Samuels."

Stanford looked down the end of his rifle. The massive beast was within his sights.

"Keep it steady," said the man. "You have to shoot it right through the front of the cranium to make sure the bullet lodges in the brain, or else it will run off like it's been bitten by a mosquito."

Stanford cocked the trigger.

"That a boy, Stanford. Topple the beast."

Stanford fired the rifle, hitting the bank of the marsh

near the elephant's feet. The sound was enough to spook the animal. It retreated back into the tall grass and disappeared from sight.

The Patron smiled. "All you need is practice, Mr. Samuels."

Stanford lowered the gun.

"Let's get back to the car."

"Will you take me to my son?"

"Keep your eyes open, Stanford. You don't want to miss anything."

The Patron slung his rifle over his shoulder and marched through the savanna until they returned to the hover car.

"Driver, take us to the residential sector."

The hover car lifted off the ground and accelerated through the savanna.

"I want you to pay attention to the surroundings," said the Patron. "Look at the splendor we have created. There is every environment you can imagine. If you don't like hunting, there are mountains to the north for skiing and climbing. If you prefer relaxing on a beach, the tropical regions to the south will suit your needs. Salus has anything and everything, satisfying all preferences. It's for you to experience."

In a matter of minutes, the land became flat; the grass and trees were replaced by rectangular fields of fertile soil with various crops.

"This is the agricultural sector. The entire population of Salus is fed from the organic produce and grains harvested here. Do you see the solar towers?"

Stanford glanced at the solar panels standing high above the fields, radiating the crops with natural sunlight.

"We were able to harness enough energy from NGC 5866 to grow crops and illuminate the civilized sectors, but we need more. We need to think bigger. That's why I recruited you. You are a big thinker, like I am."

Out the side window, far in the distance, a massive fire danced on the horizon, creating a specter of orange and red hues on the bottoms of the clouds, covered over by a blanket of black smoke.

"Those flames, Mr. Samuels, are the first step to realizing our dream."

Stanford watched the inferno spread across the distant fields like wild fire.

"Those are the fern farms. There are a dozen of them in operation and more to come. We had to bring in solitaries from outside to keep up with the demand."

"Why are the fields on fire?"

"Our scientists discovered that the ferns produce significant amounts of oxygen when they are exposed to intense heat. We are only at the beginning of our research, but it is going significantly faster than we could have hoped. We have reached the stage where we can produce enough oxygen to feed the entire population of Salus with the ferns alone. In time, we will initiate the expansion plan, transplanting ferns to the fields in the boundaries of our former home."

"You want to repopulate the colonies?"

The Patron nodded. "Salus is salvation, but it doesn't need to be forever. My legacy will be cemented when I lead humanity outside the dome, returning freedom to the people, allowing our civilization to spread across Ultim and flourish like we always dreamed we would but never had the chance. These ferns provide us an opportunity to realize this dream. I have no doubt that we will one day import enough solar energy to reset natural photosynthesis in the colonies, but until that time, the fire is our friend. It is our heat, our light, and our breath. I want you to be a part of this."

"Why couldn't you use androids in the fields?"

"You know full well that androids have a higher purpose."

"But why did you sterilize the solitaries?"

"Until we are able to go ahead with the expansion plan, Salus is our only home, Mr. Samuels. I couldn't allow incurable diseases to pass through the walls of the dome and risk all that we have left. Being in a position of authority is never easy, and hard choices needed to be made, but you must always keep the big picture in mind. I know this is difficult for you to hear, but I hope you understand that we are pushing humanity forward, not the other way around. If eliminating incurable mutant bloodlines is what's needed to advance civilization, then that's what we have to do. Those solitaries have been afforded a second chance. They no longer have to think about freezing to death all alone. Now, with these strange ferns, there is hope. The future will be different. The future will be more humane. But we can't meet the future if we aren't mindful of the present."

Stanford stared silently out the windshield as the landscape changed from agricultural plots to the tree-lined streets of subdivisions with identical houses.

"Life goes on, Stanford. Look outside. Hundreds of thousands of families continue to live full lives because of the PAD. Salus is a blessing. You won't find one person living under the dome that isn't happy to be here. You'll be happy too."

The car came to a stop in front of a house with a perfectly manicured lawn and a cement walkway leading up to the entrance. The house was identical to every other house on the block.

"Why did you stop here?"

"Just wait," said the Patron. "You needed to see the full picture. This is the final piece that brings it all together."

They sat in silence for a few minutes until finally the front door opened and a woman wearing a beige skirt and an eggshell blouse came out holding a garbage bag.

Stanford's entire body went numb as he watched the woman walk down the path and drop the bag into a trash bin on the sidewalk before making her way back up the walkway.

The woman glanced back with curiosity as she closed the front door behind her.

Stanford's voice was suddenly overcome by emotion. "Is that Sarah?"

The Patron smiled. "Now you know why I brought you here. This can be your life. You can have it all."

Stanford felt a tightening in his chest. He struggled to breathe. The copper swirled in his eyes like never before. He knew that his emotions were no longer anesthetized by the fern. His humanity had won out.

"Calm down, Stanford. Do you want me to come with you?"

"No."

"Go on, then."

The hatch popped and Stanford emerged from the hover car. He hesitated a moment to gain his composure before walking up the path. He felt as though he had walked up the very same path many times before.

As soon as he got to the door, it opened and Sarah appeared on the other side.

They stared at each other in silence.

"Stanford, is that you?"

Stanford felt the rings of Saturn overflowing with tears. "Sarah?"

She wrapped her arms around Stanford's neck. He could smell the birthday perfume. Behind her, sitting in the hallway, he glimpsed the old boy. The dog took a hesitant step forward before collapsing lazily on his belly.

"Old . . . boy . . ."

"Oh my god, Stanford, I can't believe it's you." She pulled away to get a good look at him. "Come in, please."

In the foyer, she embraced him again. Her chest heaved as she began to cry. "I thought I'd never see you again."

"They told me you were dead."

"Who told you that?"

"The scientists . . . they said they replicated you. They made you into a machine."

"Oh god, Stanford, whatever they told you, I'm so glad you found me. Please come in. There's someone who wants to meet you."

"Wait. What happened to you? I need to know."

"I was detained for a while because they thought I was infertile. But they couldn't have been more wrong. Come, I'll prove it."

A sense of excitement danced inside her as she pulled him by the arm through the living room. The room was identical to their house in the colony.

Stanford looked around to soak it all in, but he was barely hanging on.

Sarah glanced back with her perfect chestnut eyes as she led him down the hall, the dog trailing behind. "You've made me so happy, Stanford. I'm so glad you came back."

He followed her to the bedroom, also identical. On the far side, near the master bed, was a crib. Stanford stopped in his tracks and watched Sarah stoop over to pick up a child wrapped in a blanket.

"Stanford Samuels, I want you to meet your son." She approached with the child cradled in her arms.

He looked into the sleeping face of his child and felt something he had never experienced in his life. It wasn't happiness or excitement or pride or any one thing, but it was all of those in combination, surging through his body at the same time. It was a tidal wave of raw power. He was a husband, and now a father. This was his family.

"Do you want to hold him?"

"Yes."

Stanford took the child in his arms and pressed the fragile body against his breast. He could feel heat emanating from inside the wrap; little movements of the tiny feet tickled his ribs. He took in the sweet aroma of newborn skin. It was the most beautiful scent he had ever inhaled.

"I haven't named him," said Sarah. "He only arrived from the incubators yesterday afternoon. This is just as new and wonderful for me as it is for you."

Stanford looked at her. "I want to call him Sander."

"That's a beautiful name." She laughed. "He has our initials."

The blanket became moist in Stanford's hands.

"Oh dear," said Sarah. "He needs to be changed." She

took the bundle from Stanford and set it on the master bed before entering the bathroom to fetch a fresh diaper.

Stanford moved close to the bed and watched the child wiggling inside the blanket. *What an amazing thing,* he thought, *to be the father of such a precious child. This is what we always dreamed of.*

Sarah returned and peeled the boy out of the soiled diaper. "I can't believe how much comes out of such a little body," she said.

Stanford stared at the naked child while Sarah returned to the bathroom to discard the filth. In her absence, he noticed a faint scar on the child's lower abdomen. He suddenly felt faint.

Sarah reappeared and applied the new diaper. She looked at Stanford. "What's wrong, honey? You'll get used to changing diapers in no time. I don't mind doing it."

Stanford took a step back. His vision was blurry, and he felt the copper rings begin to swirl.

"Stanford, are you feeling okay? Come sit down."

"Why does Sander have a scar?"

"A scar?"

"He has a scar on his abdomen."

"Oh, they said he had an undescended testicle. It was a minor operation. It's nothing to worry about. He's fine now."

"I'm not talking about an undescended testicle, Sarah."

"What do you mean? Why are you so upset?"

"They've sterilized him. My boy has been sterilized."

"What? Why would you say such a thing? You're being ridiculous, Stanford."

Stanford felt a surge of anger. "I'm not being ridiculous. They've harmed my boy!"

"Please tell me why you are so upset."

The child began to wail through tiny lungs.

"You need to calm down," said Sarah. "You're scaring him."

Stanford leaned against the wall. He felt like he could fall over.

"I don't know what they told you, Stanford, but it's not true. They told you I was dead, too. They told you they made me into an android. I don't know why they told you those things, but here I am. We're together now. We have a child. We can make a life inside Salus. Let's forget the past and be thankful for what we have. Let's look forward to the future."

"Why did you leave me, Sarah? Tell me the truth."

She was silent for a moment. "After I was released from custody I was overwhelmed. They prodded me. The tests were invasive. I felt violated and I was confused. I didn't trust anybody."

"You didn't trust me?"

"I told you I was confused. We were struggling, you can't deny that, and I was scared. I wasn't thinking rationally."

"But you were pregnant. It should have been the greatest moment of our lives."

"I didn't know yet, at least not for sure. They told me that even if we had conceived, they needed to wait for genetic testing. They gave me the option of aborting the fetus if it wasn't eradicated. I didn't know what I would tell you."

"You thought it would be better for me if you ran away?"

Sarah's chin quivered. "I know how it sounds. I don't understand it myself. I was stupid. It happened so quickly, and I felt I needed to get away."

"Get away where?"

"I went home, Stanford. To the Perfect colony. The doctors granted me a pass. I just needed some time to clear my head. When I got there I felt ashamed so I went into hiding. I needed to be alone."

"You weren't being chased? You were in no danger?" Stanford's body shook with emotion.

"I always planned to come back. I would never abandon you. But then permanent midnight arrived. Things just happened out of my control."

Stanford leaned against the wall. "I don't know what is going on," he said. "How could you leave me like that?"

Sarah began to cry. "Please forgive me, honey. I didn't mean for it to be like this. I love you so much."

The child was wailing on the bed. Sarah picked him up and rocked him against her breast. "We are together now. I will never leave you again. You need to accept the job and stay with me in Salus."

Stanford hesitated, wiping away his tears. He suddenly felt a shiver wash over him. "How do you know about the job offer?"

"The man in the car delivered Sander from the incubators yesterday. He told me you would come. Please accept his offer. I want our family to be happy again. Even the old boy is here now. He was wandering the colony, Stanford. He was picked up and brought here—to be with us."

Stanford glanced at the old boy by the doorway, seeing the dog crouched on the floor, eyes thinning sleepily, before turning his attention back to his wife. He watched her rock the baby in her arms. The cries began to subside. He moved close and gently touched the child's soft cheek with his fingertips.

The child opened his tiny brown eyes.

Stanford snapped his hand away and back-pedaled.

"What is it?" asked Sarah.

"His eyes."

"What about them?"

"They are normal."

"Of course they are normal, Stanford. This is what we always wanted. We served the Policy."

Stanford felt his eyes getting hot. "Our child is not eradicated."

"What do you mean? Are you sick, honey? Why don't you get some sleep?"

"That's not our child. It's not Sander. I've seen my boy before. That's not him."

"For god's sake, Stanford, I don't know what's wrong with you. Please just take a nap. Everything will be better."

"I don't need a nap." Stanford's eyes began to glow. He cast a spotlight on Sarah and saw her pupils constrict to the size of pinpricks.

Sarah shielded her son from the rays. "What's happening to you?"

The sound of an explosion reverberated through the walls.

Stanford stumbled out of the room and made his way down the hall.

Sarah called after him. "Where are you going? Please don't do this."

"I'm sick of the lies."

"What lies? You've been in the desert too long. Those animals have brainwashed you. There is no conspiracy. This is reality."

"You're an android. And that's not my child—or my dog. Everything in this house is a sham."

Sarah screamed back. "Why do you think I'm an android, Stanford?"

"I can see inside you."

Sarah set the baby back in the crib and rushed down the hall after him. "If you can see inside me, you know I'm human. Please, Stanford, you're scaring me."

Stanford entered the living room and looked out the picture window. He saw a mushroom cloud rising over the fern fields in the distance.

Tears streaked down his wife's cheeks. "Don't go," she pleaded. "Please don't leave us. I beg you. I will be better." She moved close to him and held out her hand.

Stanford stared at an aluminum pendant in her palm. It was etched with the image of an owl.

Another mushroom cloud opened in the sky.

"We can be a family," said Sarah. She looked toward a knock on the door. "Please, Stanford."

Stanford approached the door and cracked it open.

The Patron stepped inside. "Mr. Samuels. A number of insubordinate solitaries have initiated a riot on the farms. We must return to the PAD for a debriefing. This will be your first operation as Executive Director."

"I'm declining the job."

"Mr. Samuels, I strongly suggest you reconsider. I've made you a very generous offer. You would be insane not to accept the position. You will be the first mutant in history to serve as the Director of the Personal Associations Division. Don't be foolish. Think about your wife and child."

"I'm not a fool. This is an illusion. You won't control me."

Sarah pleaded from behind, "Listen to him, Stanford. Take the offer. Let this be a new beginning for all of us." She moved close, wrapping her arms around his neck. "We can be happy again."

"I won't live a lie, Sarah. I already have a mission. People are dying, and I need to save my son."

Sarah came around to face him, leaning in close for a kiss. "I will always love you, Stanford Samuels."

At the exact moment her lips touched his cheek, he felt a sharp pain in his back. The pain was excruciating and brought him to his knees. He reached around and felt the handle of a knife.

Black spots invaded his vision, and when he regained focus, he saw the Patron standing over him.

"I'm tired of negotiating with you, Mr. Samuels. You have slapped me in the face for the last time. You are a mutant who dares to defy me? My face is the last thing you will see on Ultim."

The Patron aimed a gun at Stanford's head.

Sarah cried out. "No, please, don't!"

Stanford smiled.

"You smile in the face of death, Mr. Samuels?"

"No. I'm smiling because your guards forgot one thing."

The Patron smiled back. "What's that?"

"They forgot to check the toilet after the gun passed through me."

In a swift motion, Stanford reached into his back pocket and pulled out a yellow gun with a twisted double-barrel. He pressed the trigger, blowing a hole through the Patron's forehead. The wall behind was painted with thick, black fluid.

The sound of Sarah's horrified shrieks filled the room.

Just then, the driver of the hover car arrived at the front door. He scanned the carnage and reached for a weapon in his holster, firing a shot that struck Stanford in the stomach.

Stanford aimed the yellow gun at the driver and shot a hole through his face, blowing off the back of his cranium.

The driver collapsed on the front step, leaking out a pool of synthetic ooze.

The fantastic yellow color faded from the miniature handgun.

Sarah rushed to his side. "What is happening to you?" Her voice was overcome by grief. "Baby, we need to get you to a hospital. Don't you dare die on me. Stay with me, honey."

Stanford stared up at the ceiling. His body was completely numb. He turned his head to the side and saw the body of the Patron on the floor. The man's dark eyes were staring at him, as black and lifeless as they had always been. The collie approached the body and lapped the black fluid that pooled on the floor.

Stanford smiled. He felt the rings of Saturn extinguish. He heard his mother's voice from somewhere above.

Come now, Stanford. It's your time.

Stanford closed his eyes and saw the clearing in the forest. His mother and father sat on the bank. His father played fetch with the old boy while his mother cooled her feet in the water.

"Hi, son," said his father.

"Hi, Dad."

"I'm glad you came."

"I'm glad too, Dad."

"Why don't you sit down?"

Stanford approached the pool.

The old boy rushed out of the water to greet him.

"You're a good old boy," said Stanford, patting the wet fur.

His mother spoke, "We're so proud of you, honey. You are a king." Her eyes swirled and shone with copper rings.

"I could have done more."

"No, you couldn't have. You did more than your father and I could have ever imagined. You left a legacy."

Stanford looked into his mother's mutation. "I couldn't rescue my boy." He wiped away a cascade of tears.

His mother pointed toward a bank on the opposite side of the pond.

Stanford looked across and saw the assassin standing next to a prepubescent child. The child's eyes swirled with beams of light.

"You did so well, honey," said his mother. "Now you can rest."

Stanford watched the assassin turn around and lead Sander back into the tall forest of ferns.

"I'm proud of you, son. You are a king."

2.35
INAUGURATION

Clint stood in the center of the room, glancing around at the boys on the bunk beds with his most intimidating stare.

"This is the inner circle, boys. We are supposed to be in this together, but I feel dissention in the ranks. If you aren't with us, you better leave now."

Several of the boys looked at one another.

"Get out of here," yelled Clint. "If you have to think about it, then you are no longer in the inner circle."

Three of the boys stood up and made their way to the door, not daring to look Clint in the eye.

"If you say a damn word to anybody, I'll cut your heads off in the night. Mark my words."

The boys exited quickly.

Only Markus and Joshua remained in the room.

Clint smiled. "You are the strong ones. This is the inner circle. We can't break this bond."

The boys stared back in silence.

Clint began to pace. "Do you want to get out of here or not?"

Joshua spoke up. "Yes."

Clint looked at Markus. "What about you? Are you in?"

Markus nodded.

"Use your voice," said Clint.

"I'm in," said Markus.

"Okay, good. Listen carefully." Clint sat down on the edge of a bunk and spoke in a hushed tone. "My uncle is organizing an escape two days from now. When we go to the mess hall for dinner, I'll start a distraction. That's your sign to exit."

"What kind of distraction?" asked Joshua.

"You'll know. It will be obvious. As soon as I've got the attention of the robot aides, you guys need to head straight to the bathrooms on the east side. There is a ventilation shaft in the hanging ceiling. You need to figure out a way to get up there. How you do it is up to you. The shaft will take you to a barred window at the rear of the facility."

"How do we get through the bars?"

"You don't have to worry about that. If you can get that far, everything else is taken care of. My uncle has arranged for you to be taken from there. Once you exit the window, there is no going back. Do you both understand?"

"Yes," said Joshua.

Clint looked directly at Markus. "What about you, boy?"

Markus rubbed his sweaty palms together. "I understand."

Clint smiled. "In two days, you boys will be initiated into the most powerful rebel group that Ultim has ever seen. You have a chance to oppose the Patron and change history."

Markus watched Clint puff out his chest. He saw the madness behind his eyes.

"What about you, Clint?" he asked.

"I have to stay here. My job is to recruit more soldiers. Welcome to the Tech Terrorists, boys."

Markus looked at Joshua and saw the worry in his eyes. He knew he was not alone.

2.36
FINALE

An army of military vehicles was being assembled at the boundary of the encampment. Terrorists loaded the hatches of every truck with automatic weapons and high-powered explosives.

Back at the base, the assassin exited a tent and walked across the sand to another tent nearby. He entered through the flap.

Inside, the resident mother sat cross-legged, stirring a pot over a campfire, while her adopted baby slept soundlessly on a blanket next to her.

She looked up at him. "Is it time?"

The assassin nodded. "Will you be okay here? I want you to take care of things while I'm gone."

The resident mother smiled. "We'll make out just fine. We always have."

"Goodbye," said the assassin.

"Good luck, Mr. Dekkar."

The assassin exited the tent and made his way to the vehicles. When he arrived, he climbed into the lead truck. He glanced at Jack. "Are you ready?"

"I've never been more ready, sir," said Jack.

The assassin removed the transponder from his cargo

238

pants and attached it to the dash. The digital display cast a glow on the windshield. "Let's go," he said.

As the trucks proceeded through the desert toward Salus, the wild children began to appear from the darkness, moving quickly through the glare of the headlights.

"Shall we shoot them down?" asked Jack.

"No," said the assassin. "We need to keep our humanity for as long as we can."

The children came in droves, watching the procession of military vehicles churn through the sand.

Out the corner of his eye, the assassin saw the coordinates change on the tracker.

"That's the first time it's detected any movement for hours," said Jack.

The assassin watched quietly.

"Are you okay, Mr. Dekkar?"

The assassin looked at the driver. "When has anything ever been okay, Jack?"

Soon the uppermost crown of Salus was visible through the windshield. The majority of the structure was hidden by hungry, encroaching ferns.

As the military vehicles moved closer, the dome began to glow with intense hues of red and orange.

"Do you see that?" asked Jack.

The dome was like a specter in the night, the light spilling onto the desert sand like a fiery lake for miles around.

Jack spoke into the radio transmitter on the console. "Anybody get a reading on that?"

A voice returned, "Negative. The thermo-sensor is out of range. It won't register."

"Any idea what's causing it?" asked Jack.

The walls of the dome began to show signs of distortion.

Jack glanced at the assassin in awe.

The assassin remained silent.

The voice came through the transmitter again. "We believe the dome may be vulnerable."

The assassin picked up the transmitter and watched the dome through the windshield. He held the device close to his lips but did not speak.

"This could be it, sir," said Jack. "This could be our way in."

The vehicles continued toward the target.

2.37
EXTENDED

A woman in a nurse's uniform walked down an aisle through the incubators. Men in dark suits with the insignia of the PAD stitched to their breast pockets escorted her on either side. When she reached the door to the quarantine room, she paused to look back at her silent guides and then continued into the room alone.

Inside, the single capsule glowed with the digital display number 40065.

Looking about, the nurse let her hair out of a bun and approached with a wide smile. "I'm here, child," she said.

As soon as she spoke, the incubator ignited with brilliant light, bathing her soft features in a comfortable aura.

"I will care for you as if you were my own son. You have nothing to worry about."

The woman approached the capsule and looked through the glass top. "You are just as beautiful as they said you were. Your eyes are spectacular."

As she reached to open the incubator, the nurse's pupils were obliterated by the light from within. She back-pedaled to avoid the glare.

The sound of guttural grunting came from inside the capsule.

"Are you okay, child?"

Her vision was impaired by the brilliant light conditions. The capsule appeared like a luminous flashbulb to her. She looked back at the door from where she had come. A wave of panic enveloped her.

"Let me out," she said. "I can't see in here."

Her pleas were unanswered.

"Please," she yelled, beating her fists against the door.

Her cries were ignored. When she turned back toward the incubator she felt her knees buckle.

She closed her eyes but could not block out the light.

"Please, child, let it be dark."

EPILOGUE

While performing a routine patrol near the boundary of the Supernova Factory, the Extrasolar Search for Organic Life Organization (E-SOLO) detected what was initially thought to be a standard supernova remnant, not unlike hundreds of others detected on a daily basis in the region. Upon closer inspection of the unusually high gamma frequency, however, E-SOLO altered their hypothesis to allow for the possibility that the event was the result of two or more simultaneous star deaths. In the midst of tracking interstellar material to a location inside the NGC 2770 galaxy, a new signal pinged on board the research vessel, drawing the team's attention to a previously uncharted planet. The decision was made by Mission Control to dispatch a ground crew on an exploratory probe, with orders to locate the source of the alien signal . . .

Flames scorched the face of the dark surface as the descent engine settled amongst the overgrown vegetation. When the probe was firmly aground, three cosmonauts with headlamps revealed themselves from the hatch and placed their boots upon the unfamiliar terrain. Staring through tinted visors, the foreigners regarded the strange plants that surrounded them, so tall and numerous that the visitors could see nothing of the landscape beyond the clearing burned by the rocket's engine. They stood locked in collective paralysis, each visitor doubting his eyes as the monstrous ferns appeared to encroach upon the vacated probe.

Please adjust your frequency, Number One.

A cosmonaut standing a few paces in front of the others received the transmission from the orbiting vessel. The signal echoed faintly in his earpieces.

Are you under foreign influence, Number One?

The cosmonaut watched the enormous ferns through his visor. They seemed to move—to change positions—whenever he blinked his eyes. Despite spending the allotted time in the pod's decompression chamber, he realized he was still locked in a state of metabolic adaptation while his muscles adjusted to the foreign conditions. He wanted to glance back at his synthetic colleagues to see if their artificial processes were similarly sluggish, but first he raised his hand, slowly, to adjust the communication knob on the side of his helmet.

Are you under foreign influence, Number One?

The voice was louder now, rattling his ear patches.

"I . . . I am turning . . . around . . ."

The cosmonaut gathered enough power to twist his body. Out the corner of his visor he saw his colleagues standing a few paces to his rear. They appeared to be completely inert.

"Controller . . . the androids . . ."

Mission Control is attempting to make contact with the synthetics.

Facing forward took equal effort, as the cosmonaut's body was slow to regain mobility. He felt a momentary spike in blood pressure as he considered the loss of the androids. Under ideal circumstances, the mission would be aborted until a repopulated crew could be dispatched by the command center, but given E-SOLO's tendency to execute undermanned missions in the name of efficiency, the cosmonaut knew full well his assignment would be reclassified. The cosmonaut unzipped the utility pouch attached to his waist to commence standard data collection.

"I will take a soil sample, Controller."

Thank you, Number One.

With a deliberate movement, the cosmonaut removed a thin metallic rod from his pack, which expanded to a length of several feet. He dropped carefully to his knees and inserted the instrument into the spongy ground until the base-kit was flush with the surface. The rod continued to burrow into the planet's crust, reaching maximum depth before automatically retracting into the base, sealing a subterranean sample within the kit.

The cosmonaut took a moment to sift the soil through his gloved fingers. "Controller?"

What is it, Number One?

"The soil has an unusual consistency—like ash."

Perhaps from the rocket, Number One.

"Yes, Controller." The cosmonaut placed the kit back in the utility pack and got to his feet. "Controller?"

What is it, Number One?

"Has the troposphere passed screening?"

Yes, Number One. You are free to raise your visor. The oxygen is pure.

The man moved more freely now as his muscles achieved equilibrium. He depressed the same knob on his helmet used to change the frequency. Now his visor opened, exposing his bare skin to the foreign conditions. He felt the air touch his face, rushing into his nostrils and displacing the recycled oxygen from his lungs. A cool sensation filtered through his torso and petered out through his appendages.

Can you breathe comfortably, Number One?

"Yes, Controller."

Mission Control is unable to establish connection with the synthetics.

"Shall I retreat?"

No, Number One. Please proceed as if this is a solo mission.

"I can return with a new crew."

Please proceed.

"Are there risks, Controller?"

Your connection to the vessel is firmly established.

The cosmonaut looked between the inert spacemen. Their dark visors reflected his image, and behind his image he saw what appeared to be the ferns moving as if they had been disturbed by an unseen force—an animal perhaps—scurrying through the underbrush. He was slow to react due to his cumbersome spacesuit, and by the time he turned to face the disturbance, the ferns appeared naturally docile.

The cosmonaut glanced skyward, aiming his headlamp toward the uppermost fronds, but he could not detect the canopy against the black velvet sky. Somewhere, thousands of miles overhead, the research vessel orbited the dark planet—connected only by a low frequency wave to the transmitter inside his helmet. He stood in silence, the lone member of the dispatch team, breathing the oxygen created by the strange ferns that surrounded him, and wondered how they photosynthesized in the absence of natural light.

The cosmonaut stepped toward the thicket, plucking

a leaf from a low-hanging fern. The fern recoiled, emitting a high-pitched sound that punctured the night.

The cosmonaut flinched. "Controller?"

Yes, Number One?

"Did you hear that?"

Yes, Number One. Audio has been recorded.

"Controller?"

What is it, Number One?

"Requesting permission to use the organic sphere."

Permission granted.

The cosmonaut removed a spherical, palm-sized instrument from his utility belt and placed it at the base of the closest fern. He took a step back and watched the sphere flash with white light from the inside. After a moment, the sphere began to pulsate like a beating heart.

"Controller, are you receiving the data?"

Yes, Number One. Delta waves have been detected by the onboard EEG.

The cosmonaut watched the sphere pulse rhythmically for a time before the interior light changed from white to red.

"Controller, has the sphere detected beta waves?"

Affirmative, Number One.

"How can it be?"

It appears to be intelligent, Number One.

There was a pause in the transmission while the cosmonaut took hold of the sphere. The instrument went dormant as he packed it away.

Please fetch the NAV-system from Number Two.

"Yes, Controller."

The cosmonaut approached one of his inert crewmembers and unzipped the pack attached to the android's waist.

He removed a navigation device that resembled a black pyramid with a bulb on the top corner that lit up the night like a beacon. The bulb blinked steadily as it recalculated to locate the alien signal.

Beads of perspiration formed on the cosmonaut's brow. "Controller?"

What is it, Number One?

"Requesting permission to return to the probe."

Pause . . .

Request denied.

"Why has my request been denied, Controller?"

Your assignment has been reclassified as a solo mission.

"I understand. But I would prefer to return with a new crew of androids."

The androids are not able to achieve homeostasis with the planet, Number One. You require the assistance of a human crew, which would need to be authorized by Mission Control. Such authorization takes time, which we have not been granted. Your mission has been reclassified.

"Yes, Controller."

Are you compliant?

"I am compliant, Controller."

Mission Control has requested psychic imaging, Number One.

"You would like me to access the astral plane, Controller?"

Yes, Number One. E-SOLO has asked for a visual compilation of psychic impressions.

"Does E-SOLO sense the presence of latent energy?"

I believe they do, Number One.

"Am I in danger, Controller?"

You have established a firm connection with the vessel, Number One. Please apply the astral headset.

The cosmonaut felt his breathing getting rapid as he fetched the headgear from his utility pouch.

Your heart rate is 100 bpm, Number One.

"I will practice mindfulness, Controller."

The cosmonaut knew he would need to be calm to advance through the astral plane. Metabolic processes were heightened in the parallel dimension and could prove problematic for an escalated traveler. Cardiopulmonary episodes had become so frequent in the early days of astral travel that E-SOLO was impelled to adopt stringent regulations requiring human crewmembers to pass physical and mental training before achieving astral status. Due to their ability to control internal processes, androids were usually assigned the task of crossing over, but in cases such as this, where the androids ceased to function, the humans were required to access their training.

The cosmonaut took a deep breath of foreign air in an effort to self-regulate before attaching the headgear to his helmet. When the electrode pads were in place, he breathed normally through his nostrils, exhaling through his mouth. All at once, his body felt weightless.

Are you comfortable, Number One?

"Yes."

Your frequency is holding strong.

The cosmonaut glanced at the NAV-system. The bulb pulsed slowly with light.

Recalculation is complete. You may proceed toward the source, Number One.

"Yes, Controller."

The cosmonaut stepped toward the edge of the clearing. With each stride along the ashen soil, the bulb on the NAV registered a higher frequency.

The ferns were so dense that they acted like a wall designed to keep him out. He squeezed between the stalks and inched his way painstakingly through the thick forest, careful not to trip over the serpentine root system that spread like an intricate spider's web along the floor. His vision was completely obliterated now—his headlamp rendered useless by the density of the ferns all around. He saw only vegetation and nothing more. All he could do was follow the blinking bulb, which continued to pulse at a higher frequency with each step; and with each passing minute, he felt a sense of claustrophobia squeezing his lungs.

The cosmonaut struggled to regulate his breathing.

"Controller?"

What is it, Number One?

"I don't know where I am."

Your connection to the vessel remains strong, Number One.

"Why do I feel like I am losing control?"

Your vital signs are normal, Number One. Your mind is being afflicted. Have you registered a vision?

"No . . . there is only blackness . . ."

You are safe, Number One. Continue with mindfulness.

The cosmonaut advanced through the stalks, trying to focus his eyes on the blinking light. He listened to the sound of his breathing, concentrating on the rhythmic movement of his diaphragm. He visualized each cell of his body being fed by the oxygen generated in his lungs, the lifeblood circulating from his head to his toes. And he breathed the way he was taught to breathe—in through his nostrils, out through his mouth.

It was so quiet in the darkness that he felt as though he had been swallowed by the forest floor, and each step he took led farther into the center of the planet. The perpetual blinking of the bulb on the NAV was the only thing he could rely on, but it was hypnotic, and he felt his legs growing heavy, the labored beating of his heart thumped in his ears. Just as he wondered if he would ever find his way, his vision was blasted by intense light that scorched his retinas. A massive fire erupted all around, turning the plants into great mounds of ash. The flames spread quickly, blocking his return path to the research probe.

"Controller, can you hear me?" A tone of panic invaded his voice. Sweat leaked off his forehead, stinging his eyes.

I'm here, Number One. Is there something wrong?

"Can you see the fire?"

No, Number One. There is no fire. I repeat: there is no fire. You are collecting a strong psychic imprint.

"It is all around me," said Number One. He squinted his eyes against the black smoke that billowed through the stalks.

Remain calm, Number One. It cannot hurt you.

The cosmonaut felt a burst of adrenaline as he fled from hungry flames. The farther he ran, the faster the bulb pulsed on the NAV-system, until finally the bulb glowed with full power. He looked back in the direction he had come. The fire had not followed.

"Controller, the signal is static."

There was no response from the vessel.

"Controller, can you hear me?"

Receiving no answer, the cosmonaut regarded a thicket of ferns that seemed to spontaneously part before his eyes, partially revealing what appeared to be the wall of a hidden structure.

"Controller, I have found something. Is it real?"

No response.

He reminded himself that it was not unusual to temporarily lose contact when moving through the astral plane. Strong psychic projections had been known to disrupt the communication frequency.

The cosmonaut felt a shudder move through his body. He combated the fear response by utilizing his mindfulness training, concentrating once again on rhythmic breathing. When his body was sufficiently calm, he moved toward the structure and placed his hand on the wall. The surface was warm and texturally smooth. It reminded him of a gel membrane that had been heated, rendering it pliable and sticky. As he massaged the wall, he noticed that his hand was absorbed through the surface. He felt a tingling sensation on his fingertips that reverberated like a static charge all the way through his arm and into his chest. The sensation caused him to lose his breath, and in the next instant, his vision went black as he fell through space.

"Controller . . . Controller . . . Can you hear me?"

The cosmonaut's body settled upon a soft, comfortable surface. When he opened his eyes he was on a couch in an unfamiliar living room. There was a woman a few feet away, standing in front of a picture window. She was bent over, her brown hair dangling freely across her shoulders as she fed a potted fern with the spout of a water jug. The woman was completely oblivious to his presence, and he knew he could not interact with her. She was a vision projected into his brain through the headset.

He felt quite comfortable as he sat watching the woman. Beyond the picture window, he could see other houses, all with perfectly rectangular green lawns, split in half by walkways leading to front doors. A tower was visible in the distance, beaming a brilliant stream of sunlight upon the subdivision. Curiously, he saw no other people on the streets, though he imagined a city teeming with human life, much like the town he called home so many light years away. In fact, the house he had grown up in had a living room much like the one he presently occupied. He recalled looking out the picture window as a young boy, glancing around at the neighborhood and thinking about how small the world was. He wondered if his own recollections were cross-contaminating the psychic imprint.

His reminiscence was interrupted by a sound from another room. It was the unmistakable cries of a newborn child. The cosmonaut watched the woman stride out with the water jug, only to return a moment later with a blanketed bundle cradled in her arms.

As the woman rocked the bundle, the sounds of whimpering slowly faded out.

"There, there, young child," she cooed. "You will be all right. You just had a bad dream. I'm here now."

The cosmonaut watched the woman peel back the blanket to caress the child's soft cranium. Now, with the head exposed, he could see the unusual eyes that peeked open briefly before closing again in a slumber. The eyes reminded him of the spiral galaxies he had visited on countless exploratory missions with the E-SOLO team. The irises seemed to swirl and glow like millions of stars.

The cosmonaut turned his head toward the sound of knocking. From his position on the couch, he watched the woman approach the front door and peer through the peephole.

A man with a blue jacket stepped into the foyer. The letters "PAD" were stitched on his breast pocket. When he entered the living room, the cosmonaut could see that his pupils were inordinately small.

"You must evacuate," said the man, his voice absent of inflection.

"I cannot put the child at risk."

"A state of emergency has been called in the northern sector. The fires are spreading. The child is no longer safe here."

The woman glanced out the picture window. "I see no fires," she said. "I am not permitted to leave this house."

The man clutched the woman's arm, but she pulled away.

"Don't touch me, you filthy synthetic," she screeched.

Just as she backed away, a great plume of black smoke rose up in the sky, framed by the picture window. A dark shadow swept across the neighborhood in an instant.

"We have to go, now!" yelled the man.

The woman back-pedaled when she noticed that the potted fern was smoking with noxious fumes before spontaneously combusting.

Her voice was laced with terror. "What is happening?"

"The ferns!" yelled the man. "We must evacuate now!"

The cosmonaut began to choke. Black smoke was filling the room, stinging his eyes. Through bleary vision he saw the man in the blue jacket take the woman's hand and exit the front door. He could hear the sound of the child's wails getting farther away.

He stood up from the couch and approached the open door, witnessing the flames jumping across rooftops of the neighboring houses, eating their walls down to the foundations like savage beasts. Along the road, ferns sprouted from the ground in an instant, reseeding as quickly as they were converted to ash, creating a perpetual cycle that propelled the fire through the subdivision like a fiery snake. The cosmonaut could no longer see the man, nor could he see the woman with the child. Billows of blinding, impenetrable smoke moved in like an uninvited guest.

The cosmonaut slammed the door and returned to the living room. Out the window he saw a strange vision—several young, naked children ran through the yards on their hands and knees like wild dogs.

"Controller! Controller! The imprint is too strong. I am unable to self-regulate. The fire is reaching the astral plane. Requesting permission to abort!"

The potted fern sizzled in the living room.

A voice emanated from the plant. "You will not burn us."

"Controller, is that you?"

No response.

Outside, he watched the naked children running in and out of the dark plumes.

"I am hallucinating, Controller. I must leave the astral plane."

Without warning, the picture window imploded, sending a cascade of broken shards inside the house. The cosmonaut shielded his eyes before ripping the electrodes off his space helmet.

The cosmonaut screamed out: "Controller!"

He suddenly found himself standing beside the wall of the structure in the forest of ferns. His arms rested at his sides. The flames that existed on the astral plane were not here. It was quiet and dark in the dense thicket.

He watched the ferns close over the surface of the wall, hiding it once again from view. A sense of calm washed over his body as he moved back in the direction he had come. He was safe now. This place had terrible memories, and he was glad to leave. The ferns seemed to part to allow for easy travel back to the clearing. But when he arrived, the clearing was empty. The android spacemen were no longer there. And the place where the craft had been was now completely overgrown by ferns.

Suspecting he had not disengaged from the astral plane, the cosmonaut quickly reached up to feel for the electrodes, but they had been discarded.

His breathing grew rapid. "Controller, where are you? Where have you gone? Can you hear me?"

He turned his headlamp toward a flash of movement in the stalks at the edge of the clearing. Something was there. Out of the corner of his eye, a naked body scampered on all fours, disappearing before he could see it clearly. Then another evaded his sight, taking cover amongst the vegetation. He heard rustling in the underbrush on all sides. They were circling him. He was their prey.

"Controller! Where have you gone?"

The cosmonaut felt the ground move beneath his feet—a shockwave from deep within the bowels of the dark planet.

"Controller, I am hallucinating. I am stuck on the astral plane. Please bring me back."

A voice came from somewhere, but it was not the voice of the Controller. The words were faint but clearly enunciated in his earpieces. "They. Are. Coming."

The cosmonaut twisted toward the origin of the voice but saw nothing but darkness and towering vegetation. "Who said that? Who is coming?"

Another voice came from somewhere else. Again, he turned toward the source.

"The. Ugly. Men."

"Who's there? Reveal yourself!" The cosmonaut's head darted back and forth.

Overhead, the stars twisted like a spiral galaxy.

"You. Must. Go."

"I cannot go without my ship!" screamed the cosmonaut. "What have you done with it? Where is my crew?"

As if in response, the ground opened up like a mouth near the edge of the clearing, emitting a specter of red light from the depths.

"You. Will. Go. Before. The. King."

"Who is the king?"

"The. Man. With. Suns. For. Eyes."

The sound of howling exploded in the night.

"Controller . . . Controller . . . please help me."

POWER OFF

ACKNOWLEDGEMENTS

To Florence McDowell: mother, friend, and fellow author. I imagine you looking down with pride. Thanks also to Pam and Lew for providing shelter under a leaky roof, and to my editor, Jen Ryan, for her expertise and her faith in the Project. I would also like to acknowledge my most trusted beta reader, Monica, for her unwavering support. And, as always, I am grateful to Tara, for spending every day with a grumpy writer. That can't be easy.

ABOUT THE AUTHOR

Chad Ganske was born in Red Deer, Alberta, Canada, in 1976, relocating with his family to the small harbor town of Sidney, British Columbia in the late eighties. After graduating from high school he enrolled at the University of Victoria, but left after one semester to enter the workforce. Chad slogged through a variety of entry-level jobs before publishing *Idyllic Avenue,* followed by its sequel, *Salus.* He presently resides in Victoria, BC, where he spends a great deal of time alternating between states of elation and frustration while watching the Edmonton Oilers of the National Hockey League.

Made in the USA
Charleston, SC
13 March 2016